MODERN LOVE

MODERN LOVE

& OTHER TALL TALES

GREG BOYD

Red Hen Press *Los Angeles 2000*

Modern Love and Other Tall Tales
Copyright © 2000 by Greg Boyd
All Rights Reserved

No part of this book may be used or reproduced in any manner whatever without the prior written permission of both the publisher and the copyright owner.

The Stories in this book have previosuly appeared in the following publications: *Artful Dodge* and then again in the anthology *Anyone Is Possible* (Red Hen Press, 1997), "The Further Adventures of Huck, Tom and Jim"; *Asylum Annual 1994*, "Modern Love"; *Asylum Annual 1995*, "Listen"; *Fiction International 22* and then again in the anthology *Best American Erotica 1993* (edited by Susie Bright), "Horny."

Special thanks to the editorial work of Peter Pryor.

Cover image: "Franciscan Monk"
Metal sculpture by Mike Peery
Metal Maddness, Los Angeles, California

Book and cover design by Mark E. Cull

ISBN 1-888996-22-6
Library of Congress Catalog Card Number 00-100601

Published by Red Hen Press

♦ ♦ ♦

FIRST EDITION

Contents

Modern Love
1

Robot Dad
10

Listen
12

Unglued
17

Horny
22

The Further Adventures of Tom, Huck and Jim
28

Ylek, Fishing
51

The Conference
60

MODERN LOVE

Modern Love

A strange woman called me on the phone and told me she wanted to be my love slave. I asked her if she was joking, and whether she'd simply picked my number at random from the phone book. "It doesn't matter," she said. Then she told me in great detail exactly what she'd like me to do to her and the kinds of things she was capable of doing for me.

The whole time she was talking I kept looking at the blank television screen, wishing I'd had the sense to turn it on before picking up the phone. It's something I usually do when the phone goes off in the evening. That way I can watch what's on and think about something else the whole time whoever's on the other end is trying to sell me their steam cleaning or raffle tickets or whatever without having to waste my time completely or feel guilty and mean-spirited because I've been rude to them by hanging up. After all, these people usually aren't the owners of the companies or services they represent or even commissioned sales representatives, but rather temporary employees or else minimum-wage workers employed by agencies set up to perform phone soliciting services. The point is that these people have to make a living like the rest of us, and barging into the private lives of complete strangers at the dinner hour isn't exactly the kind of job a person would voluntarily choose to do. So even though I resent their intrusion, I don't want to add to the misery of someone already burdened by such a desperate situation, for I truly believe that one small insensitive act can often be enough to drive a person to unspeakable crimes. And I don't want that sort of thing—mass shootings in crowded restaurants, to take only one example—on my conscience.

So even though this woman wasn't really selling anything, I felt I had to listen to what she was saying, if only out of common courtesy. At least she had a pleasant speaking voice, though a bit husky and deep for a woman. With a voice like that I would think she could have easily been on the radio, maybe taking calls from other people. Some of what she said was very graphic and perverted. Stuff having to do with safety pins, leather goods and various body parts. You can imagine. By the end of her monologue she was breathing heavily into the receiver and whimpering a bit, which made me so nervous and embarrassed I had to get up out of my chair. Worst of all, the whole thing took a lot longer than it should have.

Finally, after she was finished, I hung up the phone. An odd electricity crackled in the air. I went into the kitchen and got myself a couple big scoops of vanilla ice cream, which I stirred around the bowl until it was soft and creamy. By the time I'd finished eating, it was raining lightly outside. The apartment suddenly seemed small and stuffy, charged as it was with static energy, so I thought I'd take a walk. My doctor tells me I should get more exercise to improve my circulation. Because I'm bald on top, I put on a fur hat to keep from catching a cold. Living alone as I do, I've often thought of getting a dog or some other small pet, but I wonder about the responsibility. Still, if I would have had a dog I would have taken it with me, maybe for protection, as this isn't the safest neighborhood, but I don't, so I went by myself, jingling my keys in my hand. I live near the cemetery, which is black in the center at night, though the sidewalk along the outer wall is fairly well lit. It wasn't much of a walk, just once around the perimeter of the cemetery. That's really about all I can take.

When I got back to the apartment the phone was ringing again. I could hear it from the landing of the floor below. I knew instantly it was mine. After all these years, I recognize the tone. For some reason I thought it might be important, even though hardly anyone but salespeople ever call, as I'm long-ago divorced with grown children I never really had a chance to become close to, who are now living in the Midwest. The few friends I once had are all deceased or else moved out of town years ago. I stayed because of my job and the pension. It's not easy to change after so many years. After making it up the stairs, I had to rush to get the key into the lock and open the door. I nearly stumbled as I hurried to pick up the receiver.

The same woman who'd called earlier was on the line. She wanted my address. "I'd like to see you now," she said. I was still breathless from rushing to climb the stairs. Finally, though, I managed to tell her I didn't think her coming over was such a hot idea. But she wouldn't give up. Then she started in about handcuffs. Apparently, she wanted me to help fasten her to my bedpost. For a moment I pictured a stranger sleeping like a dog at the foot of my bed. I wiped my mouth and the top of my head with a handkerchief. I kept saying no, over and over, but she wouldn't let go of the idea. Finally, I made up a fake address and gave it to her. She promised to be there in fifteen minutes. "Put on some water to boil so we can have tea," she said, then the receiver clicked gently. For a while I sat perfectly still and went over the conversation in my head. My hands were shaking. Finally I went into the kitchen and heated some milk to drink before bed.

Sometime during the night I thought I heard noises in the apartment and when I got up to check, my ex-wife, young the way she was when we were first divorced, was fixing toast in the kitchen, dressed only in black stockings, a garter belt, and high heels. She looked up from spreading margarine when I entered the room. "Hiya, Lou," she said, waving the knife in her hand, "long time no see."

I stared at her a long time. "Annie," I finally said, "I thought you remarried. Where's your husband?"

"Gone to a ball game. He took a cab. Say, Lou, you don't look so good. Are you getting enough exercise?" Suddenly, we were standing close together. She leaned toward me, still holding the knife. We were just about to embrace when I woke up. I'm usually not much of a dreamer, so all I could think of was the milk must have been sour.

The next morning I ate my oatmeal, took one and a half cups of coffee without any milk, and rode the subway to my office as I do every working day. Though I can retire any time, I stay on. It's what I do. Mostly my work involves tracking taxes for the same big firms, but occasionally I'm called in to consult on an annual report and sometimes I even prepare personal taxes for our wealthiest clients. I've been around a long time. People trust me, so when something big comes into the office, I'm often the one they turn to. And honestly, after all these years, the numbers kind of soothe me. That and the routine, like every day saying the same things to the same people in the morning when I come in. Or always sharpening my pencils before I sit down at my desk. At my age, people have to know what to expect.

After work I usually eat dinner at one of two places on the same block as my building. The waitresses know me and give good service without making a big fuss, which is more comfortable for everyone. They know what to expect for a tip and I know they'll refill my coffee cup twice without even asking. Both places are comfortable, not too pricey, with menus varied enough to keep me from becoming too bored to eat. At one of the restaurants they've got one of those carts loaded with sweets and sometimes, when I'm in a decadent kind of mood, I treat myself to dessert.

But that evening I couldn't seem to find anything on the menu I wanted. Finally, because a person's got to eat, I ordered a bowl of soup and a sandwich, most of which I left on the plate. For some reason I didn't feel like being around so many strange people moving their jaws, or to see women in shiny brown jumpers scurrying past, arms full of dishes. I thought I'd feel better at home where I could put my feet up, maybe watch a few minutes of television.

I'd just come through the door, hadn't even turned the set on yet, and was still unlacing my shoes, when the phone went off. "You're punishing me," she said. "Please let me see you. I want you to hurt me, but not like you did last night. That was cruel. I'll do anything you say, but please don't lie to me again." I squeezed both arms around my waist and told her I wasn't interested.

"Look lady," I said, finally, "I'm old and bald and fat and probably not much fun for you. Besides, I don't have any ropes or chains or even a ball of string around here, just a box of rubber bands, which I don't think would be much good for hand-cuffing even if I was interested in such a thing, which I can tell you bluntly right now I'm not. So why don't you try someone else, someone younger, someone with a police record?" But she wouldn't listen. Instead, she threatened to kill herself if I didn't immediately give her my real address.

"I'd die for you," she said, her voice deep and breathless. Then she described in detail how she'd slash herself with a razor blade across each wrist, up both forearms, then make another big straight rip across her neck. "I know just where to cut," she assured me. I didn't say anything. Instead, my eyes drifted back to the dull screen of the television. I don't know how long I sat there, neither of us saying a word and me just staring at the layer of dust on the convex picture tube, but it must have been several minutes. I kept hoping she'd hang up. I honestly didn't know what else to do.

When she screamed into the phone it was so loud that I jerked my head back and knocked it hard against the wood back of the chair I was sitting in. For a second the pain blinded me and I sat there blinking and rubbing the back of my head. As soon as I could speak again, I asked if she was all right. For a minute or two the line was dead silent and I started to think the worst. Then she told me in a hoarse whisper that she'd made an incision an inch deep and three inches long in her thigh with a razor blade. I shivered as she described the pool of blood that was collecting beneath her on the floor of her kitchen.

"Look lady, give me *your* address and I'll call an ambulance for you."

"No. I'm going to keep cutting myself until you let me see you. Only you can prevent it. I need your attention one way or the other. You decide."

"You're crazy," I said, but she didn't let me finish. Already she was threatening to slash her wrists. "But first I'm going to nail my hand to the breadboard. I'm not kidding," she warned, "if you don't tell me your address right now I'll drive a nail through the palm of my hand. I've got the hammer right here in my hand." She pounded it a few times to prove what she was saying was true. "Then I'll mark both my cheeks with the razor and carve your phone number into my chest."

That did it. Even though she was completely insane, I didn't want to have her death or even her disfigurement on my conscience. I didn't want nightmares of a woman with nails protruding from her body like some crazy Saint Sebastian painting or to wake up screaming in the night from seeing my phone number bleeding in pulpy flesh. I tried to tell her my address, but she said to wait until she got a pencil and paper. Then, after she'd written down the street number, she promised to call a cab and come right over just as soon as she'd bandaged her leg.

While I was waiting for her to show up I thought of calling the police and having them come up and arrest her when she got here. But what if they didn't believe me, or she told them some completely different story that made me look like a criminal? And then even if they did take her, what would my neighbors think if they saw the cops dragging a woman out of my apartment in handcuffs? There was nothing to do but wait for her.

So I sat there and imagined what might happen when she arrived. Certainly I'd manage to get her calmed down. A bowl of ice cream might divert her attention. I hoped I could talk her out of any wild schemes she might have. No doubt this stranger was putting me at great risk, but as time passed I became more and more convinced that I could handle whatever situation developed. I went into the bathroom and washed my hands and face. By now I was pacing back and forth across the apartment. Each time a car drove by, I ran to the window and looked down to the street, hoping to catch a glimpse of her getting out of the taxi. I wondered what she looked like, how old she was. Not that I cared. I only wanted something to go with the voice, something to make it real. But no taxi stopped in front of the building.

Hours passed and still she hadn't arrived. As the night progressed, I sat by the window in the darkness and the silence, the phone on the end table next to me. Perhaps she'd lost too much blood and had passed out. Maybe she'd seen that the cut was so deep that it would require stitches to stop the bleeding and had gone to the hospital. A doctor might have become suspicious and informed the police. It occurred to me that I didn't even know her name. Eventually I must have drifted off to sleep in the chair, though I remember the night was filled with red lights and sirens.

The next day I called in sick to work and stayed in my apartment. Though she'd never called me before during the day, I didn't go out for lunch, didn't even shower for fear that I wouldn't hear the phone if it rang while the water ran. As evening approached I became more and more restless and agitated. I *needed* to hear from her. But the apartment was silent. Christ, I thought, maybe she had given up on me and was making another call to someone else at this very moment. The thought made my stomach ache. At one point I turned on the television and flipped from channel to channel, image to bright image, but nothing held my attention or took my mind off of her. Evening came and went. I switched on a single light and sat in semi-darkness. Later I tried the radio, searching in vain for an announcer with a husky voice. All I found was noise, advertisements, a few stations where people talked without making any sense. I switched it off. Then I moved from room to room through the thick silence, going from couch to bed to chair and back to the couch once more.

Finally the phone rang. I bounded to it in three giant steps, snatched it up. "Hello?" My heart was racing. But it was only a salesman for life insurance. I slammed the receiver down hard and lay back on the couch with my forearm over my eyes. The city pulsed around me: a car horn on the street below, a bus accelerating through the intersection a block away. I clenched my fists and listened to the rhythmic sound of my own breathing. I sat up and touched the phone, brought it to my cheek, slammed it back into its cradle.

I wanted her. If I could talk to her again I'd tell her everything. That I wanted to strip her naked, handcuff her arms behind her back and whip her with my belt until she cried out. That I wanted to pierce her nipples with safety pins as she begged me to stop. That I wanted to wrap my hands around her throat. That I wanted her.

I got up, went into the bathroom, removed the blade from my razor and carried it back to the easy chair by the window. In the distance, I could hear the sirens. They were always present. Slowly, deliberately, I tested the blade against my neck until I could feel my pulse against the metal. My heart pounded through my ears as I lowered the blade to my lap and cradled it with both hands. For a long time I rocked slowly in the silence.

Then I picked up the phone and dialed.

Robot Dad

My mother's dead. A train slammed into her car when she stalled on the railroad tracks. I was in the front seat with her seconds before it happened. I heard the horn blow and felt the rails vibrating beneath us. I opened the door and tried to pull her out with me, but she'd frozen up completely, locked her hands on the steering wheel. I slapped her hard across the face to try to break through her hysteria, but even that didn't work. At the last possible second I bailed out, rolling onto the ground, hitting my feet and running for it. The car exploded into flames behind me on impact, throwing me a hundred feet into the air. I've never really recovered from the accident. I still walk with a slight limp, though it doesn't show when I'm doing my thing on the court. And my mother, well, you can imagine. She's long gone.

My father's not a happy man. He tells me losing her hasn't been easy for him. I guess we both get lonely. "Just what do you want me to do about it?" he says all the time. Then he reminds me that I'm not the center of the universe. "I know that," I tell him, but I can see he's not listening.

My mother's dead, I tell the priest in the confessional. He wants to know about my home life after I tell him about my stealing from stores, and the houses I've been breaking into and messing up, my drug friends, all the sex stuff. One night a band of angels dressed completely in black like Ninjas dropped down from heaven on ropes, shot her in the head with an Uzi and took her away with them. God's assassins. Who can hold a grudge? Her number was up.

Robot Dad

Once my father told me a story he made up called "Robot Dad." It was about a world where all the women got the idea to kill all the men and then convert their bodies into robots to help raise the kids and do chores around the house. He didn't explain exactly how they managed to do all that, only that the robots were machines that the women had programmed to be sensitive and nurturing like them, and they'd made them look just like their husbands did before they killed them.

What the women hadn't counted on, though, was an invasion by aliens from outer space, which happened only a little while after the robots replaced all the men. Now that there was really no one left around to defend the planet because the men were dead and the robots were supposed to be peaceful and nurturing, the aliens landed their flying saucers all over the place and stood around pointing their ray-guns until the situation was under control. Then they rounded up all the women and took them back to their planet to be love slaves, leaving the robots to watch over the children.

For a while everything went okay. The robot dads did exactly what the kids wanted. They talked like machines and said stuff like, "How about some more chocolate cake for breakfast, Johnny?" and "Would you like me to pour my coffee out so we can go lizard hunting?" No matter what happened, they never raised their voices or got mad. Pretty soon the kids started doing stuff they shouldn't and getting really out of hand and the robots didn't do anything to control them.

And that was it. The story ended just when it started getting interesting. When I asked my father what happened next, he looked at me and shook his head. "I don't know," he said.

"My mother's dead," I tell the judge. "A rattlesnake bit her in the face."

Listen

No, really, why do I even bother? You're not listening to me. And don't think I can't tell the difference. I see how you pick up your coffee cup, hold onto it, swirl what's left around inside. You aren't paying much attention so you don't hear a word I say. Why pretend? Nobody listens anymore. It's a lost art. Most conversations are so short nobody says anything. They can't. They don't remember or maybe never knew how in the first place. People bump into each other on the street, in the office, at home like us, but don't make contact. Like walking into a wall for someone like me who even bothers to try anymore. Too many distractions all around. Maybe that's the reason—radios pounding in cars, televisions flashing colors, billboards everywhere competing for attention. Even your book. I can see how much you want to get back to it, how you placed it face down on the table instead of ripping a piece of paper for a bookmark and closing it properly, how your hand, even now, right as I'm speaking about it, is trembling, almost twitching only inches away from it.

So it's certainly not me who is, like I'm almost positive you just implied, nervous or anxious or whatever. Look at my hands. Steady. I'll hold a pencil straight out if you want, something you could never do without it jumping all over the place in the air like a conductor's baton. But for me it won't waver. The point being, of course, that I'm completely focused on what I have to say, though admittedly I'm getting a little frustrated with your attitude, which I won't bother to define but will instead ask a simple, though entirely rhetorical question: "Is it too much to ask you to listen when I have something to say?" Who knows, maybe it's important. Maybe I'm just trying to find a gentle way to tell you that I've only recently found out I'm very ill—terminally ill—with galloping cancer, a brain tumor, Legionnaire's Disease, AIDS, polio, tuberculosis, yellow fever, bubonic plague, I don't know what else—or that I'm going to have a baby, something I realize we have discussed several times, but nevertheless, in spite of how we left it, never really resolved or even fully explored, no doubt because I always secretly felt that if I started to tell you exactly what I was feeling you'd stop listening.

But important as that is, it's not what I'm trying to get across to you. But I do feel that now that I at least have some partial, limited or temporary hold on your attention I can begin again to try and pick up where I was before you so rudely interrupted me with your lack of interest or concentration. But be forewarned that the second I feel your gaze or even mind beginning to wander away, no matter how slightly, like it's starting to right now, I'm going to say something else, something that's not really connected to what I want to say at all, but still worth listening to, like everything I say is, if only out of politeness and common courtesy, which will, since you seem to be in such a big hurry, only make the whole thing take that much longer.

I might say, for example, that what I'm telling you is something that's going to deeply affect your life—and the funny thing here is that even though it really is one of those super-important kinds of revelations you still have the gall to sit there with your eyes almost rolling, which they certainly wouldn't be doing if I mentioned, just in passing like I'm doing now, that I lost my job—got an envelope with the same letter inside as several others in my department saying that management has been forced to reduce overhead by eliminating key positions such as mine, which have been keeping people like you comfortable beyond what you could ever hope or expect as a result of your own work and job. Or maybe I went storming out on my own. You know I've never liked that job, the people, the whole distasteful, money-grubbing attitude in that office. Or at least I thought you knew, though now I have to wonder if you've ever heard anything I've said to you over the past year or so, or even anything since we first met nearly ten years ago. I mean really heard. Which I suppose is just another way of saying that you never really cared, or never cared enough to hear and remember what I said months or even years later.

No doubt you fooled me back then by pretending to be a good listener, which is what I most want out of a relationship and what I wish you had been and were now, and that over the years you got lazy, bored with the role, and simply let your apathy take over. And it has, believe me. In other ways, too, until what you've got to offer instead of attention is a near-total lack of sympathy, not to mention passion.

Meanwhile, ironic as it may seem, the very reason I quit my job, if that's what I'm really getting at, which, I'll tell you now in advance is not, but rather only a further attempt to force you to listen to me, was the result of being harassed by my boss at work, which, now that I mention it probably really is happening in some form or way, though it's not blatant or gross or anything. He's never tried to feel me up or ask me to go out with him, for example. But the way he looks at me—leers, really—gives me the creeps, though I'm not sure why I'm telling you this except to make you jealous, which you're not and never have been, which is why I feel it should be fairly easy to tell you about the affair I've been having or how I've been doing strip-o-grams in other offices in the building during my lunch break.

Or better still, why I've decided that sex just isn't worth the bother—all those fantasies that never seem to have much relation to what actually happens or more likely doesn't happen and then, when something finally does, the big event, it's nothing much but sweaty exercise and heavy breathing. So seeing how sex just isn't all that it's cracked up to be, not for me with you anymore at any rate, I think from now on I'll just sleep on the couch in the other room, which I should think would suit you fine as it will give you less potential exposure to someone who might try to engage you in unwanted intercourse of another nature, meaning conversation.

But you're not interested in any of this. I can see that you've got other, more important things to do, that your eyes are glazing over and look the way a child's do when he or she has a high fever and starts to imagine seeing insects crawling on the ceiling. So if you'll just excuse me, I'm not going to waste your precious time, and thank you very much for your patience and understanding. You've been awfully kind, too kind, really. Now please, just go back to what you were doing before I came into the kitchen here and sat down across from you. Pretend, if you want, that I don't exist, or that I was just coming in to refill my coffee cup, which I'll do now to help create the illusion.

Just don't ask me to continue. That I won't do. You've had your chance. And I'm resolved not to let you talk me into it at this point. Whatever I had to say will just have to wait. On second thought, I'm through waiting, waited long enough, can't wait for you not even a minute longer. I'll take what I had to say with me to the grave like some horrible secret. Bury it so deep you'll never get it out of me. So that's it, my final decision: there's nothing you could ever say or do to try and persuade me to tell you what I was going to say. I won't. My lips are sealed. Zipped. Sewn. For I honestly don't remember and will never be able to recall again what exactly I had to tell you, only that it was truly and utterly important. A matter of life and death, in fact. Something, as I said earlier, that will deeply affect our lives. But it's no use now.

Because maybe, just maybe, you were right after all about me being upset or nervous, though when you said or rather implied it, I wasn't. My hands were steady then, remember? But now I'm so angry they're shaking right along with the rest of me—so much so, in fact, that if I tried holding the pencil it would probably slip right out of my hand and hit you like a dart, with the pointed end, sharpened lead, poking right into your eye. Or my shaking hands might just grasp uncontrollably around your neck and choke tighter and tighter until you beg me to let go.

Furious, that's a better word for what I am. Pissed-off. Miffed. Burned. Outraged. Just so terribly distraught and annoyed about your lack of attention that no matter what you do, no matter what—do you hear me—whether you plead, beg, get down on your knees, whether you lose control of yourself completely and resort to threats or even the kind of violence I just spoke of, nothing could make me change my mind. No matter what.

I won't say another word.

Ungluded

People say that I'm fortunate. After all, I've pursued my career as a sculptor without the constant struggle and financial strain with which most of my peers have had to contend. In college my studio art professors praised me highly and, as unlikely as it seems, I began exhibiting and selling my work even before I had completed my degree. In the years since, critics have written flattering articles about the ironic juxtapositions and the multiple worlds I present in miniature. Today patrons pay increasingly large sums of money for my creations, galleries in major cities exhibit and sell them, even a few small museums have added them to their permanent collections. Though I am certainly not among the top rank of working sculptors, nevertheless my living (if one could call it that) is assured. Yet despite the appearance of success, I readily confess that I am a hopeless failure, a complete fraud, a pretender to my own talent, a vulture feeding on the eyes of a corpse.

As a child I was shy and sickly, largely ignored by other children. But unlike many with a delicate nature, I cared little for books. Instead, my genius manifested itself in a meticulous attention to detail and a keen interest in building. For hours I would sit by myself among my plastic blocks, creating fantastic palaces and imaginary cities. At the age of twelve I began building model airplanes, a task my patience rewarded with handsome results. I even won some contests sponsored by local hobby shops.

At first my parents were delighted. They saw how my successes helped my confidence and they encouraged me to continue. Soon my bedroom was filled with realistic-looking replicas of candy-colored hot-rods, gray battleships, red Fokker tri-planes, and camouflaged Spitfires. When I whined that I needed more space for my work, my parents obliged me by converting our detached two-car garage to a hobby room. They even gave me the key.

"I'm so happy you'll finally have room to spread out," my mother told me, though she really meant she was glad my paints and in-progress models would no longer be on constant view on a card table in the living room.

I quickly made the space my own. My father built me a large workbench and lined the walls with wooden shelves. I hung several dozen finished airplanes from the ceiling rafters and lined the shelves with plastic cars, ships, dinosaurs, military vehicles, monsters, animals and a series of anatomical models which I had special ordered from a medical supply company and two of which I was particularly proud: a human heart with all its secret valves and chambers, and a wonderfully realistic-looking eyeball. I set up my portable stereo in the room and played tapes of my favorite music while I worked, cutting molded plastic pieces from their trees with a sharp knife, sanding away the rough edges, painting in the tiniest details prior to assembling each model. I was fascinated by the properties of glue, how it seemed to eat away the plastic as it permanently fused the parts into a greater whole. Many times I witnessed this small miracle under my magnifying glass.

On weekends I ate lunch, and sometimes even dinner, at my workbench. I let it be known that I didn't like to be disturbed. By the time I was fifteen I became so protective of my little kingdom that I took to locking the door. No longer did I welcome anyone inside, not even my few friends from school. "I'm working on something really big," I told my parents. "It's going to be a surprise." By that time, of course, I'd stumbled onto the concept of synthesis and had already begun the slow, deliberate, inspired process—

the mixing, the bringing together of opposites, the seamless joining of images, the fantastic coupling that would in time become my masterpiece.

Because I had no intellectual understanding of the work and relied purely on my intuition and inspiration to guide me, I developed a kind of primitive, quasi-religious ritual. First I would select one of several tapes to play—the specific music no longer seems important, only the fact that I was surrounded by sound. Then, seated on my high metal shop stool, amid my wooden toothpicks, pots of model paint, thinner and brushes, I would carefully squeeze a large mound of clear glue onto a pie tin (early on I realized the tubes themselves were difficult to control and messy) and place it directly in front of me on the bench. Then I leaned closely over the tin, my hands supporting my chin, and stared at the glue, meditating on its colorless consistency and strong odor until I could see exactly what needed to be done next.

During this time the music seemed to grow increasingly more distinct—not louder really, but focused, intense, hypnotic—and produced in me an effect similar to that of a nocturnal animal caught in the headlights of an on-coming car. My vision, too, seemed greatly enhanced. By vision I don't mean that I could read smaller characters at greater distance or any such nonsense. Rather, I could simultaneously see details set within their widest context and could thus reflect upon the specific and the general at once. I saw, through the same lens, a black cat slinking within an entire city, a lost ring upon the vastness of the ocean floor, a grasping hand among the killing fields of history, a woman's lips hovering in the sky above the world. This remarkable facility made it so each of my choices built upon what had come before in an ever-deepening aesthetic progression. Somehow I had stumbled onto a secret world and through it discovered how beauty and love were all-inclusive; they were what held the universe together, what helped us make sense of it all.

Over a single summer my sculpture blossomed, a huge flower reaching toward the sun. I sanded, painted and fit together thousands of plastic parts from many hundreds of models. As it grew, the work devoured some of my finished models whole; others I disassembled first and incorporated piece by piece. Slowly the sculpture expanded, spreading in every direction until it filled the garage from wall to wall. I had to borrow a step ladder from the tool shed to continue work amid the swirling mass of motorcycle engines, gothic spires, dismembered limbs, railroad tracks, trolls and soldiers, pirate ships' rigging, doll house decorations, decapitated heads, military paraphernalia, animal skeletons, brick facades, steam locomotives, historical panoramas, jesters and saints, painted genitalia and other hand-carved ornaments and flourishes.

The ladder, of course, was my undoing. It encouraged me to go higher than I should have gone, to cut away at the rafters until the roof began to sag, to begin hacking through the roof itself. That's when they came for me, with loud knocks, shouting and pleading, but I wouldn't let them in. In time my father grew impatient and broke down the door. Then my mother rushed inside and wrapped her arms around me like dark wings. She was crying as she led me outside into the fierce sunlight.

Later she told me I'd been laughing and crying at the same time when they found me atop the ladder. I don't remember what happened next, except that I somehow ended up at a clinic in the country, where I stayed several days. Then I went to live with my grandmother for a while. It was a period of whispering in other rooms and great concern for my health. I slept most of the time. Whenever I asked about the sculpture people became silent and changed the subject.

When my parents finally came to take me home again they picked me up in a new car, a Cadillac Coupe de Ville. I sniffed at the new vinyl in the back seat and remembered how I had used the right quarter panel from an earlier model of the same car as a crib for the baby Jesus I had placed within the bombed out French farmhouse next to the giant football helmet and the hinged rattlesnake jaw. After he pulled the car into the driveway, my father stopped and told my mother and me to get out. "I'll park the car," he said, nodding toward the garage.

"No!" I cried, running toward the side entrance. I tested my hand on the knob and found it locked. Already I could hear the gears and a chain pulling the heavy double door. I rounded the corner and saw that the garage was empty.

It's taken me years to forgive my parents. I realize they had no idea what they were doing when they destroyed my sculpture. "We cleaned everything up," my mother explained. If only I had thought to take photos from different angles or to make detailed drawings—a schematic rendering—I might still have some hope of re-creating it. Now, however, after so many futile attempts, I can only aspire to capture occasional parts of the vision, flat sections without scope or grandness, which return to me suddenly or in dreams.

This is the bone yard of scattered fragments from which I scavenge my fortune, gather my praise.

Horny

I wake up horny. God's punishing me again, testing my endurance, so I fall to my knees and pray for strength. But evil thoughts course through my mind like a polluted stream. I try my best to purify them. I am chlorine, lava soap. I bubble and foam, but in the end it happens again anyway. It's always the same. My soul screams at the exact moment of my body's release. It's a righteous voice that wells up inside me, a deep and hoary voice that comes out of the wilderness and is filled with the indignation of the ages. It inspires in me a kind of holy terror and afterwards I shake for a good five minutes.

Though I won't eat today, I allow myself one cup of instant coffee. Then I go into the garage and give myself fifty lashes on my bare back with a leather strap. Afterwards I climb up on a stepladder and take down the cross I keep suspended from the rafters. I built it myself from heavy lumber, wood screws and angle braces I bought at the hardware store. I had to carry the beams six miles home with me in two separate trips because they wouldn't fit in or on my car. That was months ago, back when I still had a car. It was mid-summer then, and under the sun's whip the sweat dripped from my vile body as I walked and melted my impure thoughts about beach girls in their bikinis. I was already learning how to suffer.

There are leather straps on the cross for me to hold onto so that I can keep it balanced as I walk. The first few times I used it I kept dropping it on the sidewalk and by the end of the day my hands were full of splinters from trying to catch ahold of it when it started to slip from off my shoulder. Like I said, it's a very heavy cross, and long enough so that if it were put into the ground, and raised up on end with me nailed to it like it's supposed to be, it would still be plenty high to keep me way above everyone so they could see just how much I'm suffering up there. The splinters were actually never a problem, as they only added to my suffering and my contemplation thereof as I pulled them out with tweezers at home later, and it's nice for the cross to hit the sidewalk once in a while, where it makes a huge noise, though better, I think, for me to fall with it, to one knee or even right onto my face, which happens more often now that I'm actually strapped to it, but once a woman with a baby carriage was walking past me and I kind of leaned over a bit to look at her and just as I was getting a good peek the cross started to slip and only the grace of God spared her child, though the carriage was damaged beyond repair. Praise be to God.

Since then the police have kept close tabs on me. It was even their idea to use the leather hand straps. They've given me a few simple guidelines to follow as well. It's a free country, they tell me, but I'm not to bother people. And they've asked me to stay out of the mall, which is where I had a little trouble another time on account of the overzealous security officers there who accused me of disturbing people with my wild stares and weird cross annoying the young girl shoppers who mill around eating salted pretzels and sucking orange drinks through straws. The security guards wanted to grab my arms and guide me forcibly to the exit. When I refused to let them abuse my rights to freedom of religion and expression they ended up calling the police to have me arrested for disorderly conduct and disturbing the peace. Except for those two times, the police have been nice enough whenever they stop their cars to check in with me along the sidewalk downtown. There is even a young lady officer who wears her tight blue uniform shirt with the badge pinned right over her swelling chest, though none of them can keep themselves from winking at each other or chuckling. They know I'm not a criminal, but, even so, they still like to imagine I'm some kind of kook. But that laugh-about-it-all attitude is understandable given all the wickedness and depravity they witness on a daily basis.

I strip down completely and wrap the loincloth I made from an old white sheet between my legs and then twice around my waist. It's modest but authentic. I fasten it tightly at both the waist and legs with safety pins to keep the cloth from falling down and my private parts from spilling out as I grapple with the cross. I won't stand for people having any lewd thoughts or fantasies about an act that's meant to purify. And I certainly don't want to be humiliated in public. Outside I hear the wind blowing rain against the garage door as I get ready. No doubt about it, today I'm going to suffer.

On the street I see one of my neighbors, dressed in a yellow plastic raincoat, stooping to pick up her newspaper. She waves to me briefly before she scurries back inside her house, even though she knows I can't wave back because my hands are holding onto the wet straps of the cross. She's an attractive young woman who works in an office. Sometimes I see her getting out of her car in the evening, her tight skirt riding up her thighs, her high heels gleaming in the late afternoon light. Only recently married, she and her husband have lived on my street just a few months. For a second I catch a glimpse of her legs as she stoops, and I wonder what, if anything, she's wearing under the raincoat. Even at this distance I can tell that her breasts are full and round. Her big red nipples puff out and stand erect beneath the cold plastic, begging for my tongue's devotion. Her hot host is already moist with the anticipation of everlasting joy, of paradise on earth, of things to come.

Horny

But God loves me. My thoughts are interrupted by a car at the corner that splashes the cold and holy water of repentance upon me as it passes through a puddle in the road, drenching my budding lust in its wake. My hair clings limply to my head and rainwater runs down my face as I struggle against the weight of the cross, the cold, the wind that sends chilling spikes of pain up and down my legs. Sharp pebbles press into my bare feet. I pass through residential neighborhoods, and as I do I know that temptation lurks behind every door, every window. I avert my eyes, cast them downward. Along the sidewalk I see drowned earthworms that have been flushed like so many unclean corpses out from their soaked graves. Bent beneath my burden I contemplate my life and its eventual end. As the sky weeps, so do I, for my sins are great and many.

Downtown I walk past rows of storefronts, windows full of worldly goods. I don't let myself look inside or think about the shopgirls standing in their short skirts—how they pull their pantyhose up over their long legs in the morning, how they push their firm breasts into the cups of their lacy bras, how they splash perfume behind their ears and knees in anticipation. Finally I take my position at the center of town, stand silently in the rain at the intersection of Broadway and Main. People drive past in their warm, dry cars, listening to pop songs about love, or more often about love-making—the words barely clothed in a fine, see-through mesh of metaphor that leaves little to the imagination. Some of them honk their horns at me. Perhaps they know me. In better weather they might speak to me, offer me their blessing or ask for mine. More likely they recognize what I represent, why I am here. They understand that safe inside their cars they are swimming in filthy thoughts, vile debauchery.

A man and a woman in a blue Mercedes drive past slowly, staring at me with unbelieving eyes. The man wears an expensive suit, the woman a silk blouse under a tweed blazer. No doubt they've just come from a motel where they've been engaging in every illicit sex act conceivable. No doubt his penis now hangs between his legs swollen red, bruised and sore from pounding inside her tight and hungry hole. No doubt her vagina likewise feels ragged and sore from their debauch, its soft walls stretched and battered from the satanic thrashing action of the devil's massive, oversized piston. It takes a long time for the car to turn the corner, an eternity. All the while the woman looks into my eyes, first through the hysterical waving arms of the windshield wipers, then, head turned sharply to the side, through the passenger window, a harlot, a fellow sinner in need of spiritual guidance, pleading for help, for compassion. I am here for her, a beacon set firmly in place in the midst of a storm. I loosen my hand from its tether to signal and the cross slips, pulling me with it to the wet concrete. When I touch my face, my hand comes away bloody. She is gone.

I could have saved her. I could have taught her how to love. I could have taken her by the hand. I could have undressed her with my teeth. I could have . . .

By the time I get home it's nearly dark. I'm soaked to the bone, skin blue and shrivelled, feet numb and bloody, chilled, shivering, feverish. I wrap one towel around my head, another around my shoulders, a third over my legs and sit in front of the television for hours drinking hot tea and watching cable network evangelism. The first hour features a fiery preacher who explains the sufferings of Jesus for Mankind while threatening me with eternal damnation and a gospel rock singer with lips made for fellatio. Later, before my very eyes a blind woman has her vision restored by the love of Christ and a cripple walks when he accepts the Lord as his personal savior. As the camera pans the audience to show the radiant faces of the true believers

Horny

I see a pretty woman in the third row that I want to fuck. I am exaulted, mesmerized, shivering uncontrollably.

At eleven o'clock I switch off the television and pray on stiff knees in total darkness for an hour and a half. That night I go to bed exhausted and hopelessly horny.

The Further Adventures of Tom, Huck and Jim

The Usual Shit—Drought—Riches to Rags

It had been the kind of day that made his neck chaff—in spite of the slipped collar button and the loose tie—and he was heading home through rush hour traffic with a headache and an attitude. After crisscrossing the city chasing minor accounts all morning, getting stung for lunch by some publicity peon from W. F. Scott, and then jerked around for hours in the afternoon only to be curtly informed that there was no final decision yet on the new campaign his guys had worked up for one of The Big Three—in short, the usual shit—Tom was in no mood to wait for oncoming cars or anything else. His last cigarette was burning itself out in the ashtray. He needed a new pack and he needed it now. Gunning the engine of his luxury sports sedan, he slipped the transmission into gear and whipped across two lanes of traffic. Tires spinning, radio pumped up and blasting, he pulled into the over-crowded parking lot of a convenience store and double parked behind a battered white Impala.

As he exited the car and moved toward the store's entrance, Tom flipped his shades up, clicked the remote door lock, and patted his wallet through his hip pocket. Though a mid-winter evening, the air was warm and dry. A stiff Santa Ana breeze blew dust and candy wrappers across the pavement. In the distance, the mountains loomed brown and massive, their tops chopped abruptly by the dirty twilight haze.

There had hardly been a rainy day since he'd moved from Missouri six years earlier. Half that time he'd lived with water rationing regulations so strict he wasn't allowed to use the expensive automatic sprinkler system he'd installed on the new lawn at the house he and Becky bought out in the Valley. A crew of Mexicans had done the job in one day, arriving at first light with a rototiller and a truck full of rolled sod and white PVC pipe. Now the grass—Kentucky Blue—was long dead and the desert seemed to be bent on reclaiming the city. The newspapers kept calling it the worst drought of the century. Scientists predicted that if they didn't get some snow pack in the Sierras this year the reservoirs would dry up completely in the coming months. In the past they'd diverted one big river and now there was even talk of building a pipeline from Canada. Hell, maybe they could re-route the damned Mississippi while they were at it.

Somehow things had been drying up all over. When he'd first brought Becky to California not long after they were married, Los Angeles was still booming. Real estate prices had soared to unbelievable highs, defense contractors were building enough fighter-bombers and missiles to police a dozen planets, and people on the inside track were still optimistically babbling about expanding Pacific Rim trade and investment opportunities. It didn't take a genius to figure out that there was money to be made if you weren't shy about it.

Back then Tom had plunged right into real estate, signing on as an agent and taking courses for a broker's license at night while he hustled other people's listings during the day. Within a month everybody in the office was talking about how good he was. Clients trusted him, especially people with money. He made them laugh, told them stories about his childhood, complimented the wives on their looks. They liked the way he talked, his boyish enthusiasm, his home-spun humor. For him, selling big property was as simple as selling a dream. And no doubt about it, he had the gift.

Within six months he'd earned over a hundred thousand dollars in commissions and started his own office. Then he really racked it up and cashed it in, stuffing his pockets, rolling in dough, laughing all the way to the bank. Weekends when he wasn't closing yet another deal, he took Becky on all-day shopping sprees to Rodeo Drive and dressed her up like a model. When he had the chance, he picked up the house in one of the best hill sections of the valley. To celebrate, on the same day he closed escrow he bought himself a new car and one for Becky, too, insisting on ordering for her a customized license plate that read, MY BABE. Of course there were other women, too. Lots of them. Women pretty enough to star in their own television shows. He met them everywhere he went. They liked the way he talked. They liked his car, his style. It was all too easy.

But it didn't last. One of his biggest clients, a high-rolling, big-time former network television executive named Pinkston, had warned him it would eventually dry up. "Get out while you're ahead," he'd advised. He even invited Tom to come on board as a partner in a new advertising venture he was putting together. "You're good, kid. Good enough to get in on some of the action out there, to turn a real profit." But Tom, pumped up by his own success and put off by Pinkston's blustering, had just laughed him off. No doubt he'd been a fool not to jump at the opportunity. And sure enough, when the bottom dropped out of real estate six months later, Tom was stuck with huge debts and a failing business. Somehow he'd managed to save the house. But his marriage was beyond salvaging, for Becky had already left him and gone back to Missouri.

The Further Adventures of Tom, Huck and Jim

After he'd straightened out the mess—laid off his agents, secretary and receptionist, closed down the office, got the creditors off his back—he looked up Pinkston, whose agency was located in a downtown high-rise with impressive views on clear days. Since the whole business depended on creating images, the executive suites of M.T. Media were designed to impress visitors. Pinkston's own office was situated in a prime corner of the building, giving him a panoramic view of the city below. The desk and chair sat on a platform elevated a foot above the floor. "Sorry to hear about your tough luck, kid," Pinkston told him, as they shook hands. They talked idly for a few minutes before Pinkston checked his watch and made excuses about a meeting. Just as Tom was standing to go, Pinkston said, "Look, buddy, I think I might be able use somebody like you in the field. Give me a call next week."

So Tom had signed on as an account representative. That was two years ago. Since then he'd been hustling media advertising, selling concepts. It was a living.

2
The Shit gets Thicker—Robbers and Cops—An Old Friend

When Tom stepped into the store, the first thing he saw was the barrel of a shotgun. A giant of a man with long black hair, wearing a sleeveless, embroidered jeans jacket, sunglasses and a black felt hat with a feather in the headband, held the gun inches from Tom's face. Another smaller man with a short-cropped red beard stood behind the counter aiming a pistol at the head of the store clerk, who was filling a paper bag with cash from the register. Several customers lay spread-eagle behind the magazine rack, their faces pressed against the floor. "Get down on the fucking floor with the rest and close your eyes," the one with the shotgun yelled at him. As Tom eased himself carefully onto his hands and knees, he felt the cold metal of the gun barrel kiss his temple. "Hurry up, motherfucker!"

When the register was empty, the man with the pistol filled the rest of the bag with cigarettes, snack cakes, and donuts from a rack adjacent to the counter while his partner collected the wallets and purses of the customers. They also took Tom's keys. "Shouldn't park behind another car," shotgun told him, laughing. "You never know when people might be in a hurry." Then they instructed everyone to remain on the floor for ten minutes. Behind him Tom heard a woman whimpering. When he was sure the men had had enough time to start the engine, he rolled over and watched through the glass as they pulled his car out of the parking lot and turned right into traffic. The blinker was flashing and they didn't seem to be in any hurry. "Shit," he said.

Tom spent most of the evening at the police station, where a detective asked him to describe as accurately and completely as he could, exactly what had transpired during the robbery. As he talked, another officer transcribed his statement in shorthand. Next he looked through a dozen thick binders of photographs of possible suspects, none of whose faces matched those of the robbers. Based on the descriptions he, the clerk and the other victims had provided, a police artist produced accurate composite drawings of the two men. Finally, a detective who seemed to be in charge of the investigation or perhaps the whole section, asked what seemed like dozens of irrelevant questions. "Do you think I'll get my car back?" Tom said, finally.

"No telling," said the detective.

When he finally got home that night, Tom tried to call one of his tennis buddies to talk about the ordeal. No one answered. Then he tried two different women he'd been seeing, but neither was home. He even tried Becky in Missouri, but hung up without speaking when her father picked up the phone, for he was in no mood to deal with the Judge. Finally, he poured himself a whisky and sat down in front of the television. Halfway through the movie he was watching, a commercial for pantyhose aired. The camera panned across a dozen pairs of chorus-line legs kicking out at the screen, settling finally on one sheathed in hideously run nylons. "Guess who isn't wearing Hotlegs?" the voice-over asked. Then the legs resumed their dance to the tune of an insulting jingle. It was an old spot, one of the first big deals Tom had cut by himself. He'd since lost the account. In this business everything happened quickly and there was no such thing as loyalty. Tom got up and poured himself another drink. When, hours later, half-drunk and numb from the day's events, he finally went to bed, the jingle was still playing in his head.

Tom called in sick to work the next day. He spent the morning replacing his lost keys, cancelling his credit cards and arranging a car rental. He took a taxi to the rental agency, then drove to a hardware store and bought new locks for the house. The following day the police called, interrupting an important concept presentation his team had arranged to show a new client. The detective he'd spoken to before at the station told him they'd arrested someone who fit the description he'd given them and wanted him to come down to try to pick the suspect out of a lineup. "We need positive identification to hold him. It will just take a minute," the detective said. And no, he added, the car had not, as yet, been recovered.

Inside the station yet another detective escorted Tom to a screening area where, safe from view behind a two-way mirror, he could view the men in the line-up. "If you're so sure you got the right guy, then who are these other people?" Tom asked when six men entered the room in front of him.

"Just some creeps we picked up for questioning in conjunction with this and other cases. Now, take a good look and tell me. Is our guy out there?" Tom looked carefully at the six men, pausing to study each one in turn. None seemed to match the appearance of either of the two gunmen. He shook his head.

"Sorry to disappoint you, lieutenant, but I'm positive it's none of these men." Still, something bothered him about the man on the far left, a thin, worn-looking fellow about his own age. Though he was sure he wasn't one of the gunmen, Tom nonetheless felt a strong sense of recognition. "Who's the guy on the left? I'd swear I know that face."

The lieutenant shuffled the papers in his folder. "Let's see," he said, frowning. "Small-time hustler by the name of Sawyer. Huck Sawyer. Lists his occupation as an actor. Currently unemployed." The cop snorted. "No address. Brought in on a drunk and disorderly. Probably a street person." He paused and took a sip of coffee. "Why, you know this bum?"

3
Bailed Out—Huck's Tale—The Cost of Housing

On his way back from the bank, Tom wondered if he wasn't making a terrible mistake. He knew that in all likelihood he and his childhood friend had drifted so far apart that they would probably have little in common except for their past, and thus little to say to each other. Still, his conscience told him that to turn his back on someone who'd once been like a brother to him would be an unpardonable sin.

Huck looked dazed as they led him out from the holding cell. When the police pointed to who had made his bail, he stared from across the room with eyes half closed into narrow slits of suspicion. When he'd collected his billfold and pocket knife and was free to go, Huck shuffled slowly toward Tom, his head down. "Mister," he said, "I don't know you from Adam, but I'm much obliged."

Tom offered him his hand. "Tom's the name," he said. "We're a long way from St. Petersburg, Huck, but it's good to see you again."

Suddenly Huck looked up and a smile cracked across his face. "Well I'll be goddamned," he said, shaking his head in disbelief and taking Tom's hand in his own. "Say, Tom, you wouldn't have a cigarette, would you?"

Of course there was lots of catching up to do with so many years gone by, and as they got into the car and headed out of the underground parking structure, Huck soon enough persuaded Tom that the best way to go about it was with a bottle of bourbon. "This here's a fine car you got, Tom. You musta got lucky. Though you always was one for books and such. What are ya now, a lawyer?"

"Nope, just a salesman," said Tom.

"Well, I reckon everybody's got something to sell. Me, I done sold everything I own at one time or another." Tom thought better of asking him to elaborate. Instead, he told Huck about how he'd been robbed, his car stolen. "I maybe seen those fellers you're talkin' about," said Huck. "Just give me a couple of days and I'll foller 'em next time I see 'em. Then me and Jim'll get your car back for you."

"Jim?"

"Yeah, sure. You remember ol' Jim, don't ya? Me and him been on the road together pretty steady near to twenty years now. Ever since he come back from the war. Messed him up somethin' awful, that did. We seen a lot, him and me. Traveled all over. Worked in construction—shovel work mostly—back when things was easier. Then Jim gets this brainstorm and says we ought to come to Hollywood an' get us some into the movies, maybe westerns or something.

Play little parts like the guys who get shot or beat up. So we did her. Me and him both started waitin' 'round the studio gates, talkin' to the guards and shakin' hands with everyone who went in and out. Finally they run us off, but not before this one guy told us how to go about it proper. That is to read up on all the casting calls and such and to stay informed about which picture needs what kind of extras and all. And sure enough we started gettin' on. Me in a couple of commercials and Jim as an extra on all kinds of movies where they want black folks in the background. Things was surely lookin' up for us. We had us a car and a hotel room and everything we needed. They feed you meals, too, just for being there. Big spreads of stuff piled on long tables, with paper plates and plastic forks. Then one day we both got fixed as extras on the same movie. Of course there's lots of waitin' around on these sets, so Jim, he figures why not him and me slide off somewhere to blow some weed. Next thing we know they're running us off the studio and telling us never to set foot there again. But we settled in here, nonetheless. Gonna stay, too, on account of the weather."

 Tom nodded his head and pulled into the parking lot of a liquor store. He set his cigarettes on the dashboard. "I'll get us some refreshments and be right back," he told Huck. "Help yourself to a smoke if you like." When he came back to the car, carrying a bag with a half gallon of Jack Daniels, some snack food and a carton of cigarettes, Tom found Huck going through the contents of the glove box. The pack of cigarettes had vanished from the dash.

 Tom had no more set the bag down between them on the seat of the rented Cadillac and was fastening his shoulder belt when Huck cracked the seal on the bottle and took a long pull. He wiped his mouth on the dirty sleeve of his work shirt and held the bottle out before him. "That does a man a world of good," he said.

Tom frowned. "There's a law against open containers in cars, you know."

"Yeah, I know. Me and Jim done time in Mississippi once on account of that one." He took another pull and screwed the cap back on. Then he opened the carton of cigarettes and flipped a new pack onto the dashboard. "I'll just set her back in the bag and rest that down by my feet till we get where we're goin'," Huck said. "Say, we ought to go check up on Jim. I bet he could do with a snort of this here Daniels. And that way you can see our place, too. We been buildin' it ourselves. It's a ways from here, though. Out near to Burbank in the San Fernando Valley."

"You live in Burbank?"

"Well, not exactly. But nearabouts."

"I'm in Encino."

"Well that makes us just about neighbors, then," said Huck. He reached again for the bag, then thought better and pulled back, sighed, and instead grabbed the cigarettes off the dash. Huck and Tom smoked until they got on the freeway. Then Huck pressed himself against the door and closed his eyes. He snored as Tom drove.

When they descended into the valley Tom exited the freeway and reached over to gently shake his companion. Huck woke with a start, blinking his eyes and turning his head in both directions.

"Where we at?" he asked.

"Burbank," Tom answered. "How do we get to your place from here?"

"Just keep headin' straight till you get to the light yonder, then turn left and go a piece more. When you get to the river make another left and keep drivin' till I tell you to stop."

"The River?"

"Yeah. The L.A. River."

Tom nodded and turned left. "You mean that storm drain?" Tom asked, pointing to a fenced-off concrete channel. Years ago every former stream in Los Angeles had been systematically transformed into a network of wide, deep ditches collectively called the Los Angeles River. Dry most of the year, during the rainy season, these concrete channels turned into raging torrents that carried the runoff from the surrounding hills and mountains quickly to the sea.

"That's it," said Huck.

Tom made another turn and headed into a warehouse district that ran parallel to the flood control channel. "Hey, wait a minute," said Huck. "Stop the car and back up. You see that?" He pointed over his shoulder with his thumb. "There's a full sheet of half-inch plywood lying out by the curb like they was fixin' to throw it away. We can surely use a board like that. You give me a hand with it now and me and Jim won't have to fetch her all the way back on foot."

Tom turned the car around and pulled up by the curb. He left the engine running while Huck got out to inspect the wood. "Nice and straight and dry besides," said Huck, lifting it so that it set on its edge. "Now why don't you turn the car back around and we'll set her on the hood. It's only another quarter mile or so, and if you drive real slow it won't go noplace."

Halfway down the street the board slid off the front of the car, caught an edge on the pavement and ripped the driver's side mirror off the Cadillac. "Damn sorry about that, Tom," Huck said, standing in the street with the broken mirror in his hand. "But I know we can fix her up again no trouble. Jim'll know where to get another one."

4
The Great Graffiti War—In Country—Huck's Confession

"That you, Hucky?" a voice called out when they got close to the shack beneath the bridge. They'd pushed the plywood over the chain-link fence and were carrying it down the sloping concrete wall, Huck clutching the bag with the whiskey close to his chest with one hand. The board wobbled considerably and Tom had just collected a handful of splinters trying to keep it from falling. When he turned around he was staring at a man with a blanket over his head. The man pointed a revolver at Tom's head.

"Whoa, Jim, put that thing away," said Huck. "This here is ol' Tom Finn from St. Petersburg."

"No shit?"

"Straight up, man," said Tom.

"And we brought us a bottle of Jack Daniels and a nice piece of plyboard might serve as a new roof," said Huck.

Jim grinned in the moonlight, then waved the revolver in the air. "Got to be careful," he said to Tom, tucking the gun into the pocket of his fatigue jacket and extending his hand. Tom set his end of the board down and they shook hands.

"Good to see you again, man," Tom said.

"Yeah. Lotta water under the bridge," Jim laughed, pointing with his chin toward the dry channel bottom. "Anyway, like I was sayin', you never know who might come poking around here. It's a dangerous neighborhood for sure 'cause we right in the middle of a fucking gang war. Seems about every night some of them kids in big pants come down here marking their territory like wil' animals with spray paint cans." He pointed toward the graffiti on the walls of the channel. "'Bout a week back, two sets of them sprayers showed up on the same night, one either side of the bridge and us stuck here between. Pretty soon they was taking pot shots at each other to the point where we all had to clear out 'fore the police come. I thought for sure they were gonna root us out after that, but all them cops did is park their cars on the street and wait for their chopper to come shine some big-ass lights down here. Can't see nothing much 'at's under the bridge that way. We watched 'em from the sewer mouth yonder. Safest place to be, much as I hate crawling into tunnels. Reminds me of them fucking death holes in the Nam."

"I told Tom you was in the war," said Huck. He took the bottle out of the sack, uncapped it and took a pull. Then he handed it to Jim. "Jim's a hero. Got hisself a Purple Heart and every other kind of shit, too."

"Now don't get yourself started up on that again, Huck. Ain't nobody wants to hear about them troubled times. Least of all a visitor. Ain't that right, Tom?" Jim said, handing him the bottle.

The whisky burned down Tom's throat as he drank. "I don't know," he said, "might be something to hear."

"Oh, yessir, it's somethin' all right. Somethin' I'd as soon forget about altogether only I could. But you wanna hear it, I'm one for the telling." Jim paused to strike a match and Tom saw how his hand shook as he tried to touch the flame to his cigarette. "You see, two or three times a week I wake up in a big sweat, screaming my damn head off—ask Huck—the sound of AKs going off all around me. Other times I get these dreams where I'm ordered down a motherfucking tunnel at's booby-trapped. Man, I seen enough guys buy it in Nam to keep me in nightmares the rest of my life. One buddy of mine lost his legs to an anti-fucking-personnel mine with me walking not fifty feet from him. Blood soaking into the muddy grass all around him and the bunch of us standing around quiet as church not knowing what the hell we could do about it. Looked like a piece of meat chopped up on the sideboard. Dead in nothing flat. Another time I got tagged for a search and destroy and saw a head blown clear off a pair of shoulders. Christ hisself only knows all the death I seen."

Jim looked hard at Tom as he took another long pull on the bottle. "But I'll tell you somethin', Mr. College. All that ain't shit compared to what we done to them. No fucking shit. You understand what I'm sayin'? We butchered those motherfuckers. If a ville looked hostile we pulled first and asked questions later. You ever seen what a napalm strike can do to a bunch of them houses of sticks and grass? Jesus H. Christ, man. I seen kids and little babies looked like burnt toast after we went through some of them places. And that ain't all. The worst part is living with what I done myself, Lord forgive me. You see, I'm a killer, Tom, sure as our Father sits in Heaven. I shot men—maybe girls, too, for all I know—took 'em down like I was huntin' for rabbits. And let me tell you this. I'm sorry as hell for my part in it. So damned sorry that now I figure I got it comin', those bad dreams and all. Livin' like a damn rat under this here bridge is all a murderer like me is fit for."

"Aw, come on, Jim. You ain't no murderer. You was only doin' what they told you to," said Huck. "I done just as bad or worse."

"Maybe that's why the good Lord throwed us into the stew together, Huck. You ever think of that?"

"Can't say as I ever did," Huck said. "But if you'd quit huggin' that bottle like it was a new borned baby and pass it over this way, a man might have the chance to slack his thirst some." Jim handed him the whisky and Huck drank. "Now Tom, I'm gonna tell you somethin' I ain't never told nobody before 'cept for Jim, here, on account of him thinkin' he's the only blasted sinner on the face of this earth. You remember when I first lit out, don't you? I was no more than a child. I just up and disappeared one day and I ain't never been back. You wanna know why? It's 'cause I killed my own father, Tom. I killed that son-of-a-bitch, Pap."

"*You* killed Pap?"

"That's right. I know they figured it was one of them biker outfits that did him in, 'cause he had it comin' for cheatin' one of them outta his Hog in a card game. But it was me that done it. He was drinkin' every night and whippin' my ass to beat the band and I just got tired of it. So one night I laid for him and when he come in to whip me I fixed him good and that was that. I ain't never been sorry about it neither."

"He was one mean bastard, your daddy," Jim said, shaking his head. "There was plenty folks around glad enough to see him laid out."

"Well I reckon I fixed it for 'em," said Huck. "I stopped Pap for good and forever." Huck spit over his shoulder. "You think we could have some of them Vienna sausages, now, Tom? Maybe open that bag of chips and bean dip too? All this jawin' done given me an appetite."

5
An Ominous Suspicion—The Wonderful Meal—The Cave —Bad News

After Huck had passed out from drink that night, Jim told Tom a bit of disturbing news. "I didn't want to say nothin' in front of him, Tom, but Huck's not been feelin' too good of late. Been losing so much weight there ain't much left to him but skin and bone. That much you can see yourself. Most days he just want to lay around and not do much of nothin' no more. I suspicion something bad, Tom, real bad. I don't reckon he'd of told you nothing about exactly how we been gettin' on all these years, but there been more than a few times we gone hungry and cold for days on end.

That much you gotta understand. I mean such as what can drive a man to go so low he ain't even a man no more." Jim sighed deeply and fell silent, as if saying another word would cost him his last chance at salvation.

"What are you saying, Jim?" Tom asked. "This may be important."

"What I'm sayin' is that Huck done things."

"What kind of things?"

"Things for money. Things I hate to say aloud or even think about. Things no boy or man should never have to do just so we could have us somethin' to eat and a place to lie down in for a night or two. And now I'm afraid the Lord is fixing to punish him some more for it, as if the doin' weren't a bad enough whipping at the time."

Before Tom left that night, he took Jim with him in the car and drove to an automated teller machine in front of a bank, where he withdrew two hundred dollars. When he dropped Jim back at the river, he gave him the money and one of his business cards. "Look, Jim, take Huck to see a doctor. Try make sure he gets plenty to eat and, if possible, keep him away from the booze. I'll come back here to check on you in a couple of days. We can all go to a restaurant and have a good meal together. And if there's anything you need before then, call me at this number."

After Jim had promised he'd get Huck to a doctor and thanked Tom, they shook hands. Then Jim slipped through the hole in the chain link fence and vanished into the darkness.

At work the next day Tom was tired and hungover. He pushed papers around his desk, made a few phone calls, drank coffee. Every time his phone rang, he jumped. That afternoon he called on clients. After work he played tennis and tried not to think about Huck and Jim living under the bridge. He felt bad, but here was nothing more he could do for them.

Two days passed and he still hadn't heard any more from the police about his car. He called his insurance company and began making plans to lease a new Lexus. He'd almost completely forgotten about Huck and Jim when the phone rang.

"Say, Tom. We done found those robbers of yours."

"Good, Huck. That's wonderful. But I'm tied up right now. You can tell me about it later," he said.

It took several minutes to get the information across, but Tom finally arranged to drive down to the storm drain after work and pick them up. He'd promised to take them to a restaurant and now he realized, with dismay, that he'd have to. Luckily, Huck suggested they go to a coffee shop close by, where they all ordered hamburgers and coffee. Jim, winking at Tom, insisted Huck drink a glass of milk besides.

"Say, this is wonderful, eating together here like this," Huck said.

Everybody agreed. Then Jim told Tom, "We got some good news and some not so good news. First off, I seen that guy in the feathered hat you was talkin' about not a mile from our place, walkin' along the river bed. He and his buddy was each carrying something, though I couldn't tell what, on account of I was on the street above. I watched 'em crawl into one of them sewer holes. When they come out again a few minutes later, I waited for 'em to get clear of the channel, then I went and fetched back Huck. He went into that ol' sewer while I kept a look out from up above. Well, Huck, he wandered around in there a little ways, 'til he come to a kind of room down there with a ladder going up to a manhole that was padlocked shut. And sure enough, they been putting all kinds of stuff in the room for safe keeping. You tell him, Huck."

"Yes sir, Tom, there was jewelry and guns and lots of silver pots and such they'd stole from who-knows-where.

They was hidin' it all away down there. I even found this." Huck pulled a billfold from his coat pocket and handed it to Tom.

"My wallet," Tom said, opening it. The cash and credit cards were missing, but everything else was intact.

"Yeah, I figure they's probably plannin' to hit up at your place one of these days, since they got aholt your address off the drivers license."

"Well, they ain't got it no more, thanks to Jim," said Huck, laughing.

Tom said that he'd call the police and that they'd probably want to stake out the area to catch the robbers.

For a while after, no one said much. They were all waiting for the bad news to be sprung. Finally, Huck cleared his throat. "I been to see that doctor, Tom." He looked down at his plate, picked up his fork and poked at a french fry. "Well, I guess it ain't gonna go so good for me. You see, they run some kinda tests on my blood and when I called for the news yesterday the doctor told me I better get over there and talk about it. Me and Jim rode in a taxi to the clinic where this one feller tells me I got it bad. Said I'm already real sick and only gonna get worse. Said I been infected with some AIDS virus. Said I oughtta go down to County Hospital, but I told him I'd just as soon take my chances where I'm at."

6
The Bust—Law and Order—Huck and Jim on Television

The next day, acting on the information Huck and Jim had provided through Tom, the police staked out the sewer and caught the robbers red-handed as they brought in an armload each of stolen merchandise. Huck and Jim watched from behind the chain-link fence on the street above as a dozen policemen wearing bullet-proof vests and blue baseball caps dragged the two criminals, handcuffed, out of the tunnel. "Sure glad they ain't here for us," said Huck, as they watched the police shove the smaller of the two into the back seat of a squad car.

As they were poking at the bigger man, herding him into yet another car, he suddenly turned on the officers and began kicking his legs wildly, in spite of all the drawn guns. "Jesus H. Christ," said Jim, "That one's a wild feller." They watched as half a dozen police officers began beating the giant with their nightsticks. One of them ran toward him with a strange-looking device, an electric shock-gun, which knocked him to his knees. Then another officer cracked him hard across the back with his billy club and the big man fell face forward onto the street. The police continued kicking him in the ribs. Finally, they dragged him roughly up under the arms and threw him into the car.

Just then a white mini-van with a big number eight painted onto a three-dimensional billiard ball on the door pulled up beside Huck and Jim. "We just got an inside tip from a detective that two homeless men had a hand in breaking up a theft ring," a woman said, unrolling the passenger side window. "You boys the heroes who reported those guys to the police?"

"I reckon," said Huck, shrugging his shoulders.

"How about giving us an interview?" she asked, getting out of the van.

Jim scowled. "I don't see much use of us gettin' mixed up in all that," he said. "Less 'o course you offerin' to pay."

The woman tossed her hair, insulted at the mere suggestion. She was, after all, a journalist.

"I didn't figure." Jim spat on the sidewalk.

"Aw, come on, Jim," said Huck. "What's it gonna hurt?" By now the cameraman was setting up his equipment. He handed a microphone to the woman and shouldered the video unit.

"I'm Amy Lawrence, KSXY News," the woman said. "If it's okay, let's start out by me asking your names. Then I'll introduce you on camera and ask a few questions about how you helped the police apprehend the suspects. Try to forget about the camera and just act natural."

"Oh, don't worry none, Miss, acting natural comes easy to us. We both been on television and even in the pictures lots of times. We used to do extra acting all the time for the studios," said Huck. "I do believe I even got a knack for it."

That night, relaxing at home after work with a whiskey sour in hand, Tom switched on the local evening news to find news reporter Amy Lawrence interviewing two homeless men who had helped solve a rash of burglaries, robberies, and thefts. "'Tweren't nothing," Huck said, grinning into the camera. "Jim, here, done all the work. All I done is crawl into the sewer yonder and check for where they was stashing the loot. And it was our friend Tom what called the police." (Watching Huck on camera, Tom cringed. He hoped that Huck wouldn't pronounce his last name, for in spite of himself, he couldn't help from thinking he'd never seen a more pathetic and ridiculous human being.) "And then when all them police started beatin' on that big feller, I thought they was gonna kill him they was hittin' him so hard and then kickin' him all over whiles he was on the ground. I been beat a few times by the police myself, but I swear I never seen such a whippin' as they gave that poor son-of-a-bitch. Guess that'll learn him not to steal televisions and such that ain't his."

7
Mud—The River—Tom's Car—Lights Out

The rains came while Tom was on a week-long sales stint in the Big Apple. While he hustled new accounts, staged presentations, and did breakfast, lunch, and dinner with one client or potential client after another, a huge low pressure front slowly moved in from the Pacific Ocean and blanketed the entire west coast. Tom wasn't even aware of the storm until he picked up a copy of the *Los Angeles Times* on the flight back and saw the lead story concerning the record rainfall. After two straight days of torrential downpour, the hills were saturated and the runoff had turned many low lying areas into lakes. Severe mud slides now threatened several exclusive canyon housing developments and had shut down the coast highway near Malibu. From Tom's window seat, visibility was zero until the airliner broke the cloud barrier and Tom could finally see the wet and blurry lights of the city, closing rapidly below.

As he drove his newly-leased car from the airport, water rushed down the streets, pushing over the curbs and spreading like shallow rivers. Movement on the freeway slowed to a walking pace as accidents—cars that had slid out of control as they tried to change lanes, trucks that had jackknifed into the center divider or else overturned along the flooded shoulder—closed lanes of traffic. As he drove, Tom listened to reports on the radio of people in the valley who had become stranded while trying to drive their cars through an intersection in the flood control basin that normally passed for an expansive park and traffic network. Some had to be rescued in inflatable rafts as they clung to the rooftops of their stalled vehicles, water rushing dangerously around them.

As he moved his foot back to the brake pedal, he switched on his defroster. The car ahead of him crawled forward again. He lit another cigarette, and listened to the quick, rhythmic ticking of the windshield wipers. While the car was nearly new, the rubber on the wipers had been corrupted from sunlight, heat, smog and disuse, and they left wide streaks across the glass. "Bloody fucking hell," he said out loud. Nearly two hours later he had finally made it the thirty-five or so miles from the airport through the canyon and into the valley.

When he got home he knew something was wrong immediately. Cardiff Lane was all but completely blocked by cars, fire trucks, and city vehicles. Crews in yellow rain slickers and hats were on his neighbor's front lawn, shoveling a huge pile of sand into canvas sacks, while others carried them into the darkness beyond. A torrent of muddy water cascaded down the street.

"What's going on here?" he asked a fireman.

"You live here?"

Tom nodded, pointing to his house.

"Part of the hill behind collapsed and came down. We got a lot of damage already and I don't know if any of these houses will survive the night unless the rain lets up."

Inside, Tom could hardly believe what he saw. The mud had come down so suddenly, and with such force, that it had completely overwhelmed his entire back yard, filling in his pool. It had broken the sliding glass doors and covered his living room, kitchen and master bedroom with six inches of wet clay. "Jesus Christ," Tom muttered. Suddenly he thought of the river, the shack beneath the bridge. "Jesus H. Christ."

By the time he got to Burbank, it was nearly midnight. The rain was falling, if anything, even harder than before. Tom parked his car on the street above the river, pulled his jacket over his head and ran to the chain link fence. Beneath the street lights, the white water roared through the channel. Under the bridge there was nothing but water, swirling and raging.

Tom ran up and down the street calling out Huck and Jim's names, but got no answer. The rain water soaked his clothes and dripped down his face. He ran until he was out of breath, then leaned, gasping, against the fence.

Then he saw it bobbing crazily down the river channel. It approached with amazing velocity, carried weightlessly along. Yet he'd sat in it, secure in its heaviness, aware of its solid construction. Four doors, leather interior, a thousand-dollar stereo system, a goddamned burglar alarm. Loaded with all the options. His stolen car. He watched it pass by and charge beneath the bridge, disappearing on the other side. One last wild ride to the sea.

A lot of water under the bridge, Jim had said. A lot of water under the bridge.

Ylek, Fishing

I remember it as if it was yesterday. The expedition took place the morning after an extraordinary dinner party during which the maestro had, if anything, only added to his reputation as the most entertaining and distinguished of hosts. As instructed, I'd served the guests two cases of the finest champagne and tiny spiced shrimp-stuffed crêpes, each separately prepared in special molds shaped like the hands and feet of babies. No one, not the women in black gowns, their necklines adorned with pearls and diamonds that floated like lifeboats adrift on the flushed and rising swells of their exposed cleavage, nor the orchestra executives, politicians and critics in their stiff coats, dared comment on the host's seersucker tuxedo and fox-fur gloves nor utter so much as a word about the personalized organic favors which decorated each guest's plate.

It was still dark when Ylek burst into my room in a flash of sudden light, his purple hip-length waders squeaking as he walked, his fishing gear posed at the ready, his distinctive ten-inch cigarette erect in its silver holder, and shouted, "Antony, my faithful Moor, resurrect yourself at once, quit for today your flirtations with death and rise, for the fish are waiting in legions to be taken! And do hurry, as I fear the sunrise will spoil everything."

I distinctly remember sitting upright in my bed, straightening the tassel of my red velvet nightcap and checking the clock on my nightstand: it was precisely three hours after midnight. Though the maestro had never before displayed the least interest in sportsmanship or open-air adventuring, indeed had, to the contrary, often passionately and persuasively declaimed against what he called "the conspiracy and horror of the giantess nature," do not think that I was surprised, only a bit stunned by the dizzying suddenness of my climb up from the deep vault of sleep.

I rolled out of bed and reached for my dressing gown and slippers, but the maestro, passionately involved with this new undertaking, insisted: "No time for that my dear fellow," he said, tapping ashes onto the white carpet as he directed my attention to a sturdily wrapped packet at the foot of the bed. Inside, I found everything I needed: rubber boots, camouflage trousers with neatly tailored cuffs, a red chamois shirt and matching camouflage bow tie, and a canvas waistcoat with dozens of zippered pockets filled with an exquisite assortment of tiny bottles of colored salmon eggs, synthetic mosquitoes made from feathers and hooks, and innumerable lead balls of varying sizes and weights.

Outside, in the courtyard of our building, awaited a fully stocked military vehicle with massive axles and immense balloon tires, which Ylek had borrowed, along with its crew, from his friend, General Letruc. After Ylek had finished pointing out to me the particular features and merits of this armored transport, not the least of which was the 75mm canon enclosed in a fully rotating turret, we climbed into the machine, which promptly rumbled along the cobblestones and through the gate, past a man in uniform who hailed our departure with a sharp salute. Soon we were passing through one of the poorer districts, and Ylek lowered the hatch, dropping at each corner several printed leaflets, a stack of which he held in his lap. Then, after we'd crossed the Pont Neuf and turned toward the Champs-Elysées, the maestro hummed a most-impressive medley of lesser-known marches between puffs of his cigarette. *"Que la vie d'un pecheur simple doît être douce, tellement douce,"* I remember him remarking to the driver.

Ylek, Fishing

When we reached the Bois de Boulonge, we were met by a policeman on a motorcycle who escorted us past a barricade and onto a dirt road which wound its way through the grassy knolls and woodlands of the park proper. On we rolled through the forest darkness until we reached a stand of poplar trees, at which point we were diverted from our course via another uniformed agent with a flashlight. Suddenly we crashed through a makeshift hole in the underbrush and found ourselves at the edge of the *Lac Supérieur*. There the particulars of our bivouac it seems had long since been arranged, for a number of well-lit and colorful tents and pavilions, which, from their massive size, showed every indication of having once been part of a circus, dotted the shoreline, and the smell of freshly brewed coffee and baking bread permeated the chill air.

"We'll end our fast here before confronting the wilderness," said Ylek, pointing to the largest of the tents, a veritable big top, even as a platoon of workmen busied themselves unloading our provisions. "And try not to look so glum, Antony. If I'm not mistaken, your lip is quivering like that of a spoiled child who has been asked politely, but against his momentary desire, to run an errand for his poor mum. I should think a rustic meal taken in country air might even do you some good. You've had an air of constipation about you of late." Wrapped as he was in his fur cape, the maestro could hardly be expected to appreciate the degree to which one such as I, who as it had turned out was improperly, or at least not fully, attired—that is to say without an overcoat—would suffer from the elements; hence his misdiagnosis.

"As you wish, sir," I replied, my words vaporizing and floating in the chill air in front of my face, but already he was far ahead of me, fairly trotting toward the dozens of acquaintances, well-wishers, and vile hangers-on who had gathered out front to greet him, and I doubt that he heard me over the sudden fanfare of brass instruments that gaily exploded from one of the nearby pavilions.

At breakfast we encountered a number of tuxedoed and otherwise formally dressed musicians—mostly players of string instruments that had not been needed for the fanfare—who had come in out of the cold and were sitting around the banquet tables more or less engaged in card games. Though Ylek made great show of congratulating each of them—slapping the men on the back and insisting they each, regardless of their age and health, imbibe a small glass of *eau-de-vie*, and kissing the women's hands and cheeks with practiced solemnity, some of them later confessed to me in a conspiratorial whisper that they halfway resented being roused from their beds in the middle of the night for such an impromptu performance.

Always the loyal servant, I did my best to assure them that their sacrifices, like my own, most certainly did not go unnoticed nor unappreciated, and I was careful to remind them of any number of similar gatherings in the past—his staging, for example, of Orff's "Carmina Burana" in a champagne cave in Riems where the orchestra had been assembled in the largest underground grotto, the chorus lined the walls of the narrow passageways, and the audience was packed in like so many sardines in a tin against the sweating barrels all throughout the echoing labyrinth—that had at first seemed equally trying if not entirely outrageous but that nevertheless lived on in the minds of all who had participated, as well as many who had only learned of them second-hand or through accounts in the media, as memorable, remarkable, even legendary events.

Suddenly, Ylek clapped his hands together loudly and called for attention. His clear baritone voice resonating within the massive tent. When everyone was silent, he climbed atop one of the tables and began addressing the assembled entourage:

Ylek, Fishing

"First let me thank each of you, my dear friends, for joining me here in this latest installment of the joyous celebration I call life. I've taken the liberty of bringing with me several dozen cases of champagne with which to toast the ascension of the sun into the heavens, and I invite you to partake of this, my private bounty, my lifeblood, in the best of health. I've also asked some of my neighbors to join us here later this morning for what I've promised will be nothing short of a 'Bucolic Holiday' to include, among other, more spontaneous diversions, a free concert, at which I'll be conducting Handel's 'Water Music,' along with a breakfast of fresh fish, wine and warm bread. Some of you will share my pleasure in presenting this concert, as you've been selected to play in the orchestra. As for the rest of you, my equally-dear-though-nonmusical colleagues, I can only hope that during this musical feast you will be toasting my good name, enjoying the fruits of our watery harvest, or making love somewhere in this splendid re-creation of Eden. But first, my friends, we must all go help collect our bounty."

At this unexpected news, a collective murmur, like a giant sighing in a fitful sleep, filled the tent. Ylek tapped his fishing pole impatiently on the tabletop.

"Oh, now, please, there's no need to worry, as I've brought along everything we need to accomplish our recreational task: poles and reels aplenty, nets, buckets, stringers, fish eggs, fish cheese and fish ham, tackle boxes packed with every imaginable kind of hook, line and sinker. Furthermore, my dear friend monsieur Dupont, who oversees the public gardens of this, the most brilliant of cities, has assured me that the lake has only recently been abundantly stocked for the occasion. *Alors, bon pêche!*"

His speech concluded, Ylek leaped from the table and headed out into the dark hour that precedes the dawn, holding his fishing pole aloft in his hand like the eagle of an ancient legion. A sudden roar of chaotic voices filled the air, then the crowd rose up as one and followed behind him, as enthusiastic and uncertain as a noisy pack of schoolchildren on their first visit to the museum. They stopped to collect their poles and paraphernalia and hurried to find a place along the shoreline.

"Antony, cherished mahogany prince, poet of motion, won't you select something organic with which to bait my hook?" the maestro said, as I joined his side once more. Torches set onto poles driven into the sand had been lit, casting a red glow over the scene. I set off at once and Ylek called out after me, "nothing too sublime—I don't want to frighten the fish." Nearby I found a wooden cask teeming with fat night crawlers, selected with tongs what I believed to be a prime specimen, and brought it hence. When I held it up for inspection Ylek clasped me firmly on the shoulder. "I can always count on you, my friend. What would I do without you?" Then he focused his full attention on the bait. "Godspeed, brave worm," he intoned, then leaned forward and kissed the slithering creature. "Do put him on the hook now, Antony, and please, be gentle."

When I had completed the task, the maestro handed me the pole and bid me cast the line into the water. "Now see if we don't get a bite," he said, "while I tend to the champagne," then disappeared into the darkness. All up and down the shore of the artificial lake I could see men and women in evening dress baiting hooks and casting lines. At the extreme end of the pool several groups of people were engaged in launching rowboats.

By now, a faint streak of gray had appeared in the sky as an intimation of the coming dawn and I knew that Ylek would be busy distributing glasses to the many guests. For some reason, I felt foolish holding onto a pole to which was attached a string to which was attached a hook upon which I vividly imagined a crucified worm was twisting beneath the water, so with mixed feelings of guilt and relief I left the fishing pole on the sand and began serving magnums of champagne.

I admit that I was anxious to see how the others were making out, so it was with a certain glee that I approached the first group of fellow anglers. "Champagne, sir?" I asked. He shook his head no.

"I'm in no mood for celebration," he replied sullenly. I noted in a glance that his feet were wet and muddy and he had somehow managed to wipe bait of some sort all over the front of his tuxedo trousers.

"No luck?" I asked.

"Not even a nibble."

And so it went all up and down the shoreline. Here someone had slipped and fallen into the lake, there someone else had put a hook through her finger, and still no one had managed to catch even a single fish.

When the sun finally made its appearance it was greeted by a weak and uninspired toast. Ylek, of course, was furious, though, as always, he remained philosophical. "What do these fools expect? I create for them the atmosphere of a carnival and they complain about the cold, the deprivation of sleep, the stains on their shirts, the lack of fish in their baskets, all the while refusing to laugh, refusing to join me in a toast to the sun." He turned to me. "Do you plan to die someday, Antony?"

His question hung in the air and I paused for a moment before answering, "Yes, of course, maestro."

"You know, my friend, I think that we are all perhaps too comfortable at times in our little suits of skin and bones. We should try to remember that life is not a dull dinner party, but rather a feast, a celebration that is over far too soon."

Just then a captain of the gendarmes approached and informed us that a huge crowd of unruly people had entered the park and was rapidly approaching on foot. Though reinforcements from every *arrondissment* had been summoned, it was doubtful that the mob could be contained. "What will we do?" I cried out.

"Please, Antony, control yourself," said Ylek, "champagne, captain?"

I was indeed beside myself with terror: "When they find out . . . Surely there will be a riot!"

But Ylek had already turned away and was striding purposefully, called forth, no doubt, by some mysterious inspiration. I looked at the captain, who was pulling on his moustache, his brow furrowed with worry. He hunched his shoulders, then shook his head sadly.

Then I heard the scratchy sound of a diesel engine cough once and come to life. Off in the distance, the maestro had perched himself atop our military vehicle. As the tank rumbled into position along the shoreline Ylek waved his arms and called out for everyone to clear the lake and move to a safe distance. When the area was vacated and the fatigued musicians, partygoers, cooks and workmen were standing together on the grass overlooking the lake with glazed yet bulging eyes, the turret of the tank rotated toward the water, canon barrel rising as it swiveled.

Suddenly the artillery piece fired off a round that rocked the ground we stood on and nearly sent the maestro toppling. Voices cried out in terror as the shell landed in the middle of the lake and exploded underwater. A tremendous geyser shot into the air. Then the armored vehicle turned and ambled up the grassy slope, Ylek waving happily as he rode. It came to a halt before us. "Captain," Ylek called down, "Can you handle a boat?"

The captain hunched his shoulders again and looked blankly at me. "Do you know how to row, to manipulate the oars?" Ylek tried again.

"Yes, of course," replied the captain.

Ylek, Fishing

"Excellent. Then you two climb aboard and the sergeant here will take you to where the boats are moored. And Antony, if you'll be so kind as to collect the fish that are now floating on the surface of the lake while the captain propels you, we'll get on with our little celebration."

We scrambled aboard even as Ylek himself was disembarking. As we pulled away I could see the maestro shaking hands with his concertmaster and a short time later, from the middle of the lake, I heard the orchestra tuning.

And so you see, that is how Ylek, while conducting his orchestra in concert (oh, to have a recording of such a performance!) earned the reputation as the greatest fisherman in France.

The Conference

Next to me on the kitchen table, set neatly on a plate to catch the blood, is my landlady's head. As soon as the water on the stove comes to a boil I'm going to drop it into the pot and make soup. It's not that I want to underscore some point about anarchy, or social injustice, or how the end doesn't justify the means. All that's been done before by writers whose names I'm quite sure you'd recognize and who I know you'd agree I could never equal. Besides, I've been warned that that kind of thinking beforehand only leads to dull and didactic expression. And it's not that I'm hungry either, though I'll admit there were times during the week I spent at the conference that I was forced to go a day or two, maybe longer, though it's difficult to say for sure, given the conditions I was subjected to, without any food. Nevertheless, the sole reason I'm serving the head up so ceremoniously here is that I want you to read what I've written. And my teacher told me there's no better way to begin a story. "The best stories always include decapitations," I remember him insisting.

He'd been critiquing one of my workshop pieces, a story about a young man who seemed to have everything going for him—a full athletic scholarship to a good school, a beautiful and talented girlfriend, a place in his father's business when he graduated from college—but who felt somehow that he wasn't in control of his own destiny, that he was making the choices others expected him to, that his whole life had somehow been laid out from start to finish as neat and easy as the clothes he used to find folded on a chair next to his bed in the morning as a child. "This is lifeless,

The Conference

boring, stupid, mundane, thoroughly knee-jerk-thoughtless rubbish," my mentor had told me, waving the story in front of my face. For a second I thought he might even slap me with the pages. "A real slice of whining post-adolescent shithole life. Why, oh why, do I even bother?" he asked. "Would somebody please fucking tell me?" Then he took another sip of beer, wiped his mouth on his sleeve and set the bottle back down on the table.

He rubbed his eyes and looked at me, as if for the first time. Then he smiled almost warmly and chuckled. "Ah, but that's not to say there's no potential in it," he said. "Sometimes all that's lacking is an emotional connection. A moment of honesty and clarity. An epiphany, if you will, though I've never really understood exactly what the hell that word means. At any rate, I recommend you give it some head. Really, trust me on this one, John: What's a body without a head?"

It was the second day of the conference and he was drunk again. "It's Roger," I reminded him.

"Now don't get defensive," he told me, reading my face. "A writer's got to have a tough hide, a thick skin, a coat of mail, a bullet-proof vest, a trick knee, a hard head, a numb skull, a fat lip, a glass jaw, a tin ear, a sharp eye, a mind of his own, a banana in his pocket, a long rope, and a rubber ass for all the times he gets kicked. More importantly, he's got to be able to do whatever it takes to make things work. You understand what I'm getting at?" I nodded. "Okay, then get yourself another beer before you go back to your typewriter. You must know where they are by now. I've taught you that much." I got up and opened the refrigerator. "And bring me one, too," he mumbled.

The refrigerator was crammed full of bottles. I pulled out two more, opened them and set them down on the table. He lit another cigarette, ripped my story in half and laughed. "Just drop a head somewhere in this damn thing.

Better still, put it at the beginning and start over. You're going to find it's terribly liberating."

I took a tiny sip of beer and stared at the floor. It was ten o'clock in the morning and my head was already spinning. When I got up from the table to excuse myself I saw that the conference director's head lay sideways on the table. His mouth dangled open. As I backed away he began to snore. I stumbled out the kitchen door and into the backyard, where I fell into a chaise lounge all but buried in the knee-high weeds. A rusted swing set towered in the near distance, next to a dilapidated wooden fence like some ominous torture wheel transplanted from a Bosch hellscape. I closed my eyes to shut out the blight and felt the sun burn into my eyelids, the sweat roll down my neck. Then I drifted into a restless, tortured sleep—the sleep of the lost, of the damned.

◆ ◆ ◆

I'd first seen mention of George Body's so-called conference in an ad I encountered in *For Writers and Poets*, a magazine I'd borrowed from my Creative Writing professor at the university. Not that I'm officially in the writing program or even an English major. Far from it. Actually, I'm a Business Administration major with a specialization in Accounting. But I've always imagined myself writing stories or maybe even a novel someday, so when I got the chance I signed up for a course in writing short fiction. At first my girlfriend thought I was crazy. "Where are you going to get the time for that?" she'd asked me. "You're already so busy with your other classes and with Basketball practices and team travel that we hardly ever spend any time together as it is."

The Conference

But Tammy's a great gal, a cheerleader and biology major to boot, and after she'd seen some of the stories I wrote she began to encourage me to write more. Once she even told my father over the phone that we couldn't come to mom's birthday dinner because she had to study for a big test when really it was me who didn't want to go on account of the story I was in the middle of writing. And believe me, my dad's not easy to handle, though Tammy knows how to wrap him around her finger.

And my professor thought the stories I wrote for the class were pretty good, too. I made copies for the workshop and, after Dr. Harder pointed out the realistic manner in which my characters seemed to communicate, just about everyone in the class complimented me on the skilful way I handled dialog. Actually, it was Dr. Harder who first planted the summer writing conference seed and then watered it, initially with his guarded enthusiasm and later with his tears, as it were. We'd talked about it once or twice when he'd gone over my stories at meetings in his office. But I have to admit, the whole idea kind of intimidated me. Most of the programs he showed me brochures from seemed so high-pressure and professional, not to mention expensive, with lots of best-selling or big-name writers in residence, that I secretly felt I'd stick out like a hammer-struck thumb.

So I was particularly pleased when I ran across the advertisement for The Suburban Writer's Conference. I felt like I had discovered, purely by chance and completely on my own, a familiar and intimate environment in which I could feel comfortable building my skills as an apprentice fiction writer. Instead of being held at some prestigious east-coast university in Massachusetts or Connecticut, or some fancy retreat in the mountains of Vermont or New York, the ad for the SWC flatly stated that both the workshops and the dormitories were located in "a 1950's vintage suburban housing tract half a block from tennis courts and the unremarkable campus of Carmen Miranda Junior College." Compared to other programs, the fees seemed modest, the staff and number of visiting artists small and the student-writer to mentor ratio low, the latter guaranteed by extremely limited and selective enrollment. Before returning the issue of *For Writers and Poets* to Dr. Harder, I wrote a letter requesting more information about the conference.

The information packet, which included a brochure with a photograph of a nondescript little house with a flat roof, a short biography and photo of the writer and editor George Body, the conference's founder and director, and a list of facilities and visiting writers who would be in attendance for the two-week summer session, arrived within the week. Looking at the photo of George Body made me want to study with him: though he was the author of a number of critically-acclaimed books as well as the editor of an independent literary journal called *PapaDadaBlastFurnace*, he seemed completely at ease, unlike so many of the faces, those portraits of pretension, I'd seen displayed by writers affiliated with other such programs. To me Body seemed loose—not happy, but relaxed—as though he'd just finished writing a novel and could finally stare off at nothing for a while. It was a calm I imagined only a writer could earn and then experience. Also included were an enrollment form and a request for a writing sample, plus details about how potential student participants were to be selected. The promotional materials all stressed that the program director was committed to accepting only student writers with "an as yet undeveloped but nevertheless remarkable gift."

When I showed these materials to Dr. Harder and asked his opinion about which of my stories to submit as a sample of my writing he was strangely subdued, as though disappointed that I'd uncovered and chosen a program without his help. I thought he might be sulking because a number of his associates were scheduled to be visiting writers at various other programs around the country and his lover was the director of one of the lesser-known conferences in New England, a program he'd recommended to me highly on both of the previous occasions we'd discussed my attending a conference. "Well, I can't say I'm familiar with the guest faculty," he said, flipping through the promotional materials, "though I do know of *PapaDadaBlastFurnace*, though I've never read any of Body's work. I'm surprised you don't try to get into the conference at Sycamore. One of my more advanced students, Peter Stringer, has already been accepted there. I know you'd enjoy working with Arthur Bongo Beauchamp, who, for my money, anyway, is one of the most distinguished short-story writers of his generation as well as a close personal friend." But I'd already decided to apply to the Suburban Writers Conference. I needed only to pick my sample.

Eventually, with Tammy's help, I settled on my story "Bad Connection," which is composed entirely of dialog between two people talking on the phone, one of whom has dialed the wrong number but because of heavy static on the line neither can hear clearly enough to realize it and once they do both continue the conversation because it's too embarrassing not to, for the sample, though my first instinct had been to go with "The Party," a sad piece about a divorced woman whose son keeps asking her embarrassing questions like "Why are your legs longer than the other kids' moms?" and "How come when daddy left he put his fist through the wall?" and "How come you don't have a job but wear so much pretty jewelry and lipstick?" and "How come men come over in the middle of the night and go into your bedroom, make gorilla noises then leave?" and "How come Tommy says 'Nina and her friends are horse?'" because he's bored, resentful and somehow suspicious that it's her fault he wasn't invited, along with all the other kids, to a neighbor kid's birthday party.

Tammy had favored "Love Bites," which has always been her favorite. It's about a teen-aged girl who comes to realize that the hickeys her boyfriend wants to give her all over are slowly draining the blood out of her body. As she begins losing weight and eventually her strength as well, her parents worry that she's suffering from an eating disorder and take her to a doctor who tells them that it's nothing to worry about, that she's probably just experiencing a late growth spurt. After they leave, the doctor turns to his nurse, a very thin and pale young woman, reaches his hand up under her skirt, and begins kissing her, then sucking on her neck. When he unbuttons her dress, there are dozens of hickeys covering her chest. "Gross!" Tammy yelled out loud the first time she read it.

Three weeks later I was delighted to receive a letter of acceptance to the conference, signed by none other than George Body himself. The letter stated that he wanted to thank me personally for my interest, and that my work displayed a fine awareness of how random events influence narrative. Best of all, though, he was looking forward to working with me closely during the duration of the conference. I was so excited I felt lightheaded for a moment. Then I ran from the mailbox up the stairs to my apartment, wrote out my check for half the tuition and called Tammy to tell her the news.

After the third ring a woman's voice said "hello" and for a second I thought that Tammy must have been taking a nap. I started right in about how I'd been accepted into the conference and when I paused she said, "that's wonderful, Johnny." That's when I realized that in my excitement I must have dialed the wrong number. "How's your mother?" the voice asked.

"Mom's fine," I answered.

"And your sister?"

The Conference

"Same as always," I replied, though I don't have a sister.

"Is she still living all alone with her little boy? What's his name?"

"Roger."

"Yes, little Roger. It's such a shame about her."

"A real crime."

"She isn't in any trouble is she? With the law, I mean? Oh, it's so sad. Isn't there something we could do . . . to help her?"

"We've tried. She won't listen."

"Oh, I know. It's just that I feel so bad. And your poor mother. How she must feel about all this I can only imagine. You know, Johnny, I've never said this before because I never wanted to interfere. It's none of my business, I know, but I've always felt that something strange happened with that doctor. You know, the one who was treating poor Nina for that rash—those terrible red marks—or hives that she had. She was never the same after that. Do you think he could have done something? You know . . ."

As I listened I'd been slowly reaching my hand around to find the phone jack. I grasped the little clip between my thumb and forefinger, said, "Listen, . . ." and yanked it suddenly out from the phone. Then I inserted it once more and called Tammy.

"That's great," she said when I read her the letter. "I told you those stories are killer. I can't wait to tell everybody."

"Look, Tammy, just don't mention any of this to my folks. I still don't think they're ready to understand how serious I am about writing. Maybe in a few years when my novel's been on the best seller list for a dozen weeks I'll mention something about it to the old man. Until then, though, I'd rather keep the whole thing under wraps, if you know what I mean."

"But what are you going to tell them? I mean you can't just take off for weeks and not tell them where you're going."

"I'll say I'm going to visit Yosemite. That they can find themselves. It's on all the maps."

♦ ♦ ♦

I arrived in the city of San Sebastian on a mid-July afternoon after a two day bus ride, my backpack weighted down with dictionary, thesaurus, half a dozen spiral notebooks, a pair of high-top basketball shoes. The bus station was located in what passed for downtown—at an indeterminate point along the three mile commercial strip that bisected the surrounding housing developments. The sun was blazing ferociously and there were few people on the street. I went inside the station to inquire about a taxi. "Carmen Miranda College," the man behind the counter repeated, "it's not too far. I'll call a taxi."

A few minutes later a white Toyota with a dented side panel and a detachable plastic sign on the roof, the same kind pizza delivery people use but this one reading TAXI, pulled into the parking lot. The driver didn't get out, so I opened the back door and threw the pack inside. Then I got into the front passenger seat. There was no meter. "What's the fare to Miranda College?" I asked.

"Five bucks."

"How about to Nerval Avenue, near the college?"

"Five and a quarter."

We headed down the main street, passing several shopping centers along the way. While stopped at a red light, I saw a man walking along the sidewalk carrying a large wooden cross on his back.

The Conference

"Nice town," I said to the driver. "I just arrived, never been here before. I'm going to a writer's conference."

"Oh," he said.

Ten minutes later we pulled to the front of the house pictured on the promotional brochure. It looked the same, except that the lawn had been neglected. I paid the driver six dollars and dragged my pack from the back seat, across the overgrown grass and up the front steps. There was no bell, so I knocked.

When no one answered, I knocked again. Tired, thirsty, my back wet with sweat, I gave the door a solid pounding. I was just about to give up and sit down on the stoop when a voice yelled from inside, "Just a minute. Hold your fucking pants on." A minute later I heard the lock turn and the door opened. Before me stood George Body in a bathrobe.

"I'm sorry," he said, "I was asleep." He looked as if he'd risen not from a nap but from the dead. His face was gaunt and covered with a stubble of beard, his eyes were puffy and red, and his was hair tangled and dirty. The blue terrycloth robe he was wearing was missing its belt and beneath it he was visibly naked: his penis hung like an undersized fish from a stringer. He held out his hand. "You must be Roger. To tell you the truth, I wasn't expecting you this early."

We shook hands. "If you don't know by now, I'm George Body. Welcome to the anti-Paris, Roger. Jesus, it's hot out there. Come on inside and I'll get us both a beer. Then we can sign you in and get you settled." I followed him inside and stood in a living room overwhelmed with books. They lined the walls from floor to ceiling and spilled out in piles that grew like potted plants in the corners. Magazines and still more books covered the coffee table. "Have a seat, Roger," Body said, handing me an ice-cold beer. "Relax."

Signing in, it turned out, consisted of my handing over a check to cover the remaining half of the tuition. Getting settled meant throwing my pack in the spare bedroom, a tiny space with faded white walls, a single mattress on a metal frame, an old office chair and a student desk with a manual typewriter, six sharp pencils and a ream of white paper on its top and a plastic trash can underneath. "It's a small house," George called out from his bedroom as he was getting dressed, "but plenty big enough for guests." He promised to search for a pillow and sheets just as soon as we'd sat down together and finished another beer.

We talked for a few minutes about my bus trip to San Sebastian and my general impressions of the town. I was just about to ask when the other conference attendees and guest writers would be arriving and where they'd be housed, when George suddenly jumped to his feet and excused himself. "Look, Roger, I've just remembered something important I must do. Please make yourself at home for an hour or so. I'll be back in time for dinner." Then he hurried out the door. A moment later I heard the sound of an engine coughing and sputtering, followed by a tremendously loud exhaust noise. I looked out the window to see an ancient green Volkswagen beetle with George Body behind the wheel, farting out the driveway in reverse, like some crazy wind-up toy. A moment later it was halfway down the street.

By the time he returned I was reading one of his novels which I'd found on the bookshelf. Entitled *Mermaids Singing*, it was about an old man who plans an escape from the nursing home where he's been sent to die. He's loaded up with pain medications and can barely move. But in his mind he plays out all kinds of tender memories from his youth, memories of a woman he loves. Tears roll down his wrinkled face. Somehow he gets the idea that he must find her. He also has a craving for sardines in tomato sauce. For

The Conference

days he plans how to get out of bed and begins discarding his painkillers, stashing the pills in his pockets or under his bed, pouring the liquids into his bedpan. After a while the pain returns, slowly sharpens, begins to define his existence and give him the edge he needs. He senses that anything is possible, slides the covers off and pulls his legs over the side of the bed, touches the floor with his feet. He puts on a robe and slippers, then shuffles to the door. It's very early in the morning, sometime between shifts of the nursing staff. A few women in white uniforms are standing together by a coffee maker, eating donuts and talking. Taking tiny steps, he stumbles down the hall to the lobby, passes the empty reception desk. It takes all the strength he can muster to push open the front door. Suddenly he's standing in the sunlight.

For a few minutes he stands on the sidewalk in front of the building and watches the cars go by. He sees people pass by on their way to work. He wants to touch each of them, to take hold of their hands, to press his lips to their cheek. He wants to reassure them, to point out the color of the sky, to tell them their love, whatever they feel, is not in vain.

At the corner he sits down to rest on a bench. A bus pulls over, comes to a jerky stop. The automatic doors open. He climbs the stairs and grabs hold of the railing. As the bus pulls back into traffic, the driver asks for his fare. He reaches into the pocket of his robe, drops a couple of tranquilizers into the bin and sits down in the seat nearest the exit. The driver glances over his shoulder and glares at him. "What the fuck?" he says.

The old man looks into his eyes. "Sardines?" he asks.

"Hey, Pop, I think you'd better get off at the next stop," the driver tells him.

"Yes," he says. "Thank you, Johnny."

When the bus pulls over he descends. He follows people into a huge building, which turns out to be a shopping mall. Somehow he ends up in the lingerie section of a department store . . .

Before I could read any more, Body came through the front door carrying two grocery sacks full of quart beer bottles. "You want to give me a hand unloading this stuff?" he asked. I put the book down, slipped my shoes back on and followed him out to the garage. The car was loaded with provisions: eight cases of beer, two half gallons of Jack Daniels, several cartons of generic cigarettes, a grocery bag full of hamburger, franks and various cuts of red meat, a sack of oranges, three two pound tins of coffee, and a case of pork and beans in the can. I suddenly realized he'd gone out to cash my check before the banks close.

"Now we're all set," Body said, as we stored the last of the beer in the refrigerator. "You hungry? I'll make us some steak and beans."

That night over beer and Jack Daniels on the rocks, the writer finally made me understand that there would be no other students. "You mean I'm the only one who applied?" I asked.

"Heavens no, there were others, lots of them in fact, but you're the only one I accepted."

"But why?"

"I can't take money from people I can't help."

"And you think you can help me?"

"We'll see. I think I can try, anyway."

"So there's no one else coming at all?"

"Well, I can't say for sure. Usually one or two people tend to drop in. I expect this time won't be different."

"But no one else is enrolled."

"That's right, it's just you and me, baby," he said, slapping me on the back. " 'Nother beer?" He brought two more to the table. Then he shook two cigarettes from his

The Conference

pack, put them both in his mouth and lit them. When he handed one to me, I tried to wave it off, to tell him I don't smoke. "Look pal," he said, "just hold the burning stick in your hand a minute, then tell me you don't want it. There'll be plenty of time for suffering in this life. Tonight we're gonna enjoy a couple of quiet drinks and a good smoke. Tomorrow we start work."

That night I slept in my clothes on a bare mattress with no pillow. I dreamed I'd had myself committed, had signed papers declaring myself to be mentally incompetent, had entered an institution, an asylum where I would be locked away, a place where I would, in effect, henceforth spend my days finger-painting alone in a white room as big as an airplane hanger. George Body was both my painting instructor and the chief psychiatrist. "Put your whole arm into the paint can." He grabbed me by the wrist and forced my hand into a five-gallon tub of red paint. "Now have a Valium," he said, popping a pill into his mouth like candy, then holding another out to me. "Relax." Suddenly choral music began to fill the up the immense empty space. It grew louder and louder . . . I woke up to the sound of a typewriter accompanied by what I later learned was Fauré's *Requiem*, one of the dozen pieces Body plays when he's writing. I put on a light and searched for my watch. It was just after five in the morning.

◆ ◆ ◆

I woke up the second time that day to the sound of my writing teacher singing in the shower. It was a painful sound, like an animal caught in the steel jaws of a trap. At first I thought he'd scalded himself, and I jerked myself upright in the chaise lounge. But as the howling continued, I collapsed back on the chair and wiped my brow against the shoulder of my T-shirt.

A fly buzzed on my sweaty neck and my mouth felt as though some sadistic dentist had packed it full of gauze and x-ray film. Lying coiled in the weeds I found a garden hose. I opened the spigot and let the water run. When the water had cooled a bit I rinsed my mouth, drank down several swallows and spit the rest. The warm water tasted of rubber and minerals. I held the hose above my head and let the liquid flow over my face and run down my back and chest. After shutting off the spigot, I opened the side gate and walked around to the front of the house, where I leaned against the garage in the shadow of the eaves.

Across the street was a nearly identical house with several cars parked on the lawn. A number of people—men with beards wearing muscle shirts, faded jeans and baseball caps, young girls with long skinny cigarettes in hand and droopy made-up eyes, barefoot kids in filthy t-shirts and diapers—were milling around. People walked in and out of the house. The front door remained open and loud music emanated from within. From time to time, one of the men would poke his head under the open hood of one of the cars while another sat in the driver's seat and cranked the ignition. As I watched, another car pulled into the driveway and two more men got out. "Fuck you," I heard one of them say, by way of a greeting.

By now, George Body had no doubt finished his shower and was wandering around the house in his blue robe. But I couldn't face him. I felt certain that he'd either force me to drink another beer or sit down at the typewriter. Just the thought of him suggesting I "try another draft" was too much for me, so I turned up the street and headed for the tennis courts. A couple of kids were volleying against the wall. Suddenly I longed for nothing more than to get inside a gym and practice my jump shot.

The Conference

    I walked across the campus, heading for the largest building I could see. In the lobby of the gymnasium I paused to drink from the cooler by the entrance. Again, the water tasted strongly of minerals, though this time it was at least cold enough to drink. I swallowed enough to make my stomach ache, though my throat still felt parched. For a moment I thought I might faint, throw up, or both, so I crouched down by the trophy case and put my head between my legs. I wondered if I was suffering from heat stroke from sleeping face up in the midday sun. After several minutes I felt better, good enough at any rate to stand again and made my way through the double doors and into the gym.

    Most of the floor had been covered with canvas tarps and a tall scaffolding on wheels had been pushed up against the bleachers on the wall nearest me. The whole building smelled of chemicals and the walls and part of the high ceiling were newly painted a fresh coat of white. I walked out a ways to look at the facility, stared up at the ceiling, and glanced around. Near the center of the room were several large drums of paint, some coiled orange electrical cords and what must have been a compressor. Just as I was about to turn back toward the exit, a man in painter's coveralls entered through the locker room door at the opposite end of the gym, walked quickly toward the paint drums and thrust his arm into one of them. When he pulled it out again he was holding something shiny. "Forgot the tape measure," he called out to me. Then he hurried back the way he'd come and disappeared again behind the doors.

    Outside the building I retched into a plastic-lined metal trash can. As I straightened up again I noticed a pretty girl holding a camera. When I looked at her she turned away, and I thought she must have snapped a photo of me being sick. She was walking away from me and I started after her. I imagined catching up to her, grabbing her roughly by the arm, taking the camera from her and ripping the film out. She moved away quickly. "Hey," I called out, but she ignored me and disappeared into the doorway of a building marked FINE ARTS in block letters.

Eventually I came to an area with outdoor tables and a phone. A few students sat together in groups of two or three, talking about their summer classes. Others sat alone reading books. I dug in my pocket for change and called Tammy. We talked until my money ran out, which wasn't very long. After I hung up the phone I felt better, like I'd got something off my chest. I wiped my eyes and went into the cafeteria to buy something to eat. I don't remember what I ordered, only that it tasted pretty much like the food I'd been used to eating at the university. Institutional cooking, I guess it's called. But somehow, like hearing Tammy's voice on the phone, it was familiar and it comforted me.

As I was eating, a cooling breeze blew up and shook the leaves on the trees. When I finished, I walked around the little campus some more, stopping to poke my head inside the library. After digesting my food I headed back toward the gym and then out onto the playing fields behind it, where I found a running track. As I was already wearing cross-training shoes, I decided to jog a few laps to help clear my head. After a mile or so, I felt good enough to pick up the pace. I ran the fifth mile hard and finished with a quarter-lap sprint. Then I headed back to the house on Nerval Avenue. Now that I'd recovered a bit, I wanted nothing better than to do what Tammy had suggested, to confront Body and get my money back, maybe even head out to Yosemite on a night bus if one was running. I strode along at a good clip, my hands clenched into fists, my arms swinging at my sides. I was pissed.

Body had told me when I first arrived that he never locked the door and that I should feel free to come and go

The Conference

as I pleased, so when I got back to the house I barged right inside. I found him sitting on the couch in the living room watching a television talk show. "Hey, Roger," he said, turning to face me. "How's that story coming along? Take a seat if you like and let's talk about it."

For a second I was taken back. The television surprised me. "What are you watching?" I asked.

"Tristen Meyers. It's research for a novel I'm writing. But I'd be happy to turn the sound down while we discuss your work."

"Listen, Mr. Body," I began.

"Please, I told you to call me George. Or call me "asshole" if you prefer. But in any case drop the formality. It's bad for my nerves." He must have been reading my mind.

"Okay, George," I said, trying to control my voice. But already I could feel my nerve slipping. "I've got a few questions."

"Fine." He smiled. "Sit down and I'll do my best to answer them." He gestured to the chair next to the couch and I slid into it. "What's it like out there, anyway?"

I stared at him. "What's it like? What do you mean, what's it like? What in the hell are you talking about?" I could feel the emotion tightening my voice box like a fist squeezing a parakeet, could feel the blood rushing to my face.

George Body smiled again, and spoke gently. "The weather. What's the weather like outside?"

I looked away. "Oh," I said, lowering my voice. "The wind has come up. It's getting cooler."

"Good. Then it will be a fine night to work. But first let's get back to your questions. Please."

Suddenly my tongue swelled in my mouth, the way it had whenever I'd been called upon to answer a question the semester I'd taken a beginning French class to fulfill one of my general education requirements. I scrambled for words. "Well, first off," I stammered, "I'd like to know . . . just where are these guest writers you advertised."

"Oh they're right here in the house," he said. "You've already met them both." I stared at him again. "My cats, Max Shocraft and Maureen O'Toole, two first-rate poets. Anyway, their essence, natural grace and savagery is far superior to most of the verse I see published these days."

I shook my head and stared down at the floor. I was trying my best to seem disapproving.

"Listen, Roger, I admit that I can be both playful and threatening. But it's always been my intention to suggest that a lot more goes into this process and product we call fiction than you'd previously imagined. That's why I thought you wanted to come here, or at least that was why I selected you as my student. From the letter you wrote and the story you sent I suspected that you were a good deal less polished and hence potentially more open to the truth than the average Master of Freakish Attitude writing seminar type. But now I can see from what you're saying, and certainly from what you're repressing as well, that you're wondering just what the hell you've got yourself into. No doubt you signed on with a completely different set of expectations for this whole experience and now that this one week out of your young life doesn't seem to be on the exact course you thought you'd charted, you're ready to mutiny, lock the captain in irons, and row away in the dinghy while he goes down with the scuttled ship. Not that I'd blame you, of course. If you demanded I give back what little remains unspent of your money and left here tonight in a fit of self-righteous indignation you wouldn't be the first student of mine to have done so. Far from it. And if that's what you plan to do, I can accept your decision and live with your misguided anger, knowing that it has nothing to do with me."

The Conference

He picked up his cigarettes from the coffee table, tapped one loose from the pack, then offered one to me. I shook my head no. I watched him strike a match, touch the flame to the tip of the paper and draw the smoke deeply into his lungs. "By the way," he said, exhaling smoke through his nose, "have you eaten yet?" I told him I'd had dinner while I was out. "Well, then, there's nothing left but to have a drink in the kitchen while I tell you how I wrote one of my best stories. Come on," he said, waving me up and out of the chair.

I don't know why I followed him into the kitchen. Maybe it was just easier to go along with it a while longer than to make a big fuss. I watched as the writer got two beers out of the refrigerator, opened them, handed one to me. "Thanks," I said.

Body leaned against the kitchen counter and drank down several gulps of beer. Then he looked at me with his head cocked slightly to one side. "You know something, Roger. I get the feeling that you don't trust your source material, that for some crazy reason you think you've got to spend all your time pulling situations out of your blessed imagination." He laughed wildly and took another swallow. "I'll tell you why that amuses me. It's because that same imagination you place so much value on is largely made up of little bits and pieces of stories other people have been telling you. Stories about what it's like to be a man, stories about the ideal society, stories about what you should expect, even stories about what it means to be a writer. Now the sooner you realize that your imagination isn't really your own, the sooner you can discard those stories other people tell you every day and find some newer, more interesting ones to work with. And they're not hard to find, because stories are in everything, Roger, everything." He was talking faster now, and progressively louder, winding up for God-knows-what kind of *Bolero*-like finale. "There are voices locked inside the minds of people and the essence of things all around. You just have to listen. It's that easy. Listen and you'll hear them. Then you can write them down."

I didn't know what to say, so I nodded in response, then pulled on my own beer as he continued. "The subject matter is life and it's everywhere, in everything. And that means dog shit, dirty dishes, and jock itch just as much as it does love, war and death. You've got to look at everything, every fucking thing. Do you understand?" Before I could answer, he grabbed an empty beer bottle from the counter and smashed it down against the edge of the sink so that it shattered into pieces. Then he dropped the bottleneck into the sink as well and walked over to me, holding his arm out in front of him.

"You see my wrist?" He wass almost yelling now. He brought the arm closer, waved it under my nose so that I could clearly see the raised white welt of scar. He paused a moment and looked so deeply into my eyes I feared he might locate and commit some unspeakable crime against my soul. "When my wife left me seven years ago I thought I was going to die," he said, finally. He lowered the arm and turned back to stand near the sink full of broken glass.

"You see, I loved that woman . . . still do, and her walking out on me was the toughest damn thing I've ever had to come to terms with in my life. Christ, not that I blame her for leaving—no more than I'd blame you for packing it up and getting back on the first bus out of here. I wasn't any easier to live with back then. If anything, I was worse: more distracted and detached, a lot angrier, scared to hell and back most of the time, uncertain, worried. You get the idea. And of course we didn't have a pot to piss in either. I dragged her from one damned place to another. Sometimes I think we must have lived in half the cities in the world. She supported me for the most part, working in banks, doing secretarial jobs, whatever she could find. The woman believed in me, for God's sake. And I had no idea what it meant to love the way she did."

"So I fucked it all up, flushed myself and my life right down the john." He paused and took a tiny sip. Then he licked his lips and set the bottle carefully down on the sideboard, just out of arm reach. "I was getting pretty desperate and started hitting the sauce," he said. "I'd been writing for twelve years, been married for six, and hadn't published much of anything. A few stories in magazines that didn't pay, an appearance in an anthology, and one little prize of five hundred dollars was all I had to show for my work. Editors in New York didn't know me from Santa Claus, I didn't have an agent, and I wasn't even fit for janitorial work. So I started feeling sorry for myself. I went from writing during the day and drinking at night to drinking all the time and complaining. I started hanging around bars and talking too much. I stopped listening completely. When my wife needed a new dress to wear to work, I bitched about it. I bitched about everything, took out my frustrations on the people around me. Pretty soon friends stopped calling. Christ, some writers I'd corresponded with for years even stopped answering my letters. Then I crashed the car, got my sorry ass thrown in jail. And still I wasn't done."

He lowered his head and closed his eyes for a moment. "I'm afraid this old, sad story makes me very tired," he said. He was speaking slowly now, almost softly. "One day Janet came home from work to find me dead drunk, burning my manuscripts on the floor of the living room in the apartment we were renting. Fortunately, I'd put a big pot, the one we used to make spaghetti, on the carpet, or I'd have probably killed myself and burned down the whole building. Anyway, I'd spent the worse part of the afternoon drinking gin and methodically igniting each sheet of several unpublished novels with a cigarette lighter, then dropping the flaming papers into the pot. I can still remember thinking it was great fun. Several had fallen astray, so there were burn marks and ashes all over the carpet from where I'd had to stomp them out with my feet. And that's the gay and magical little world into which my wife entered, simply by turning a doorknob. She left me that same night.

"I remember laughing, laughing, for crap's sake, as she packed her things. I was hysterical, completely berserk. I laughed her right out of the apartment and threw the gin bottle at the door after her as she closed it. It was that funny. Then I went back to burning what was left of my manuscripts. A week later I was still drunk. Nothing mattered or made the least bit of sense to me. Eventually, though, I ran out of money, which meant that I couldn't buy any more booze. That's when I realized just how serious things had turned. Not only was I thirsty in a big way, but there was nothing much left to eat, all my clothes were dirty and the apartment was completely trashed.

"For a while longer, a couple of days, I'd guess, I just sat around and stared at the walls. I smoked cigarettes and took long naps. Finally, I managed to take a shower and shave. Then I called up perhaps the only friend I had left and asked him to send me enough money to get me through the month. I started reading the want ads in the newspaper each morning and eventually I found a job as a night watchman, which allowed me to pay the rent, wash my clothes, and eat. But all during that time I was missing Janet so bad it was like someone had stuck a hot poker down my throat and another up my ass. I couldn't move without hurting. And I knew there was no way she was ever coming back.

"One day about six months later, I'd just started washing the dishes and was reaching my hands in beneath all the suds to find the scouring pad when suddenly the whole sink started turning red, even the soap on top. I must have been careless loading the dishes in the sink, for a glass had broken and I'd slashed my wrist pretty deeply when I'd plunged my hand into the warm water. The funny thing is I didn't feel a thing. In fact, I stared at the sink for several seconds before I realized why the water was red.

"When I pulled my hand from the water I saw that the blood was oozing steadily, in waves almost, from a nasty-looking lip of skin. Though I was scared shitless, I managed to wrap a clean dishtowel around my wrist and put pressure on it with my other arm. But it was still bleeding, so I took myself to the hospital. After they'd stopped the bleeding and taped the wound, the people in the emergency room wanted to know exactly how the accident had happened. When I told the nurse, I remember she looked at me very closely, then asked me some other, seemingly unrelated questions. Finally she told me I'd have to wait to speak with another doctor before I could leave. It was only at that point, as I waited for the resident psychologist to arrive, that I realized I wasn't entirely sure I hadn't cut my wrist intentionally. I also realized I had to write the whole thing down.

"As soon as they released me, I went straight home, called in sick to my job and wrote it all out on a yellow pad with my left hand. That was the first story I ever sold to a paying market. It's called 'Glass.' A year later I sold my first novel and a story collection. With the advance I made the down payment on this place and started the magazine. And I've been struggling hap-hap-happily along ever since."

George Body reached for his beer and took a long drink. "Well, I realize that's not exactly an answer to your unasked question, but somehow I figured you wanted to know just what in the hell gives me the cheek to call myself a writer. So now you've got my story. Now all that remains is for you to give me yours." Body smiled one of his aggravating and enigmatic smiles. Then he proposed we each adjourn to our separate studios and begin work in preparation for the following day's session. We were just leaving the kitchen when he turned to face me. "Oh, yeah, one more thing," he smiled, "while you were out this afternoon, a friend of yours, Samuel Harder, phoned. One of your professors, he said. It seems he's now in San Francisco guesting at some writing event or another and asked if he could stop by for a visit on his way to L.A. He said we should expect him sometime around noon tomorrow."

I followed Body down the dark hallway, entered my room and shut the door behind me. Slowly, as if in a trance, I slipped a sheet of paper into the typewriter and sat down at the desk. A minute later *Carmina Burana* erupted on the stereo in the adjacent room. Then I heard a staccato sound, loud and fast, like a weapon being fired on full automatic, bang through the walls as keys slapped the platen of Body's typewriter. I sat perfectly erect in my chair and listened for a long time to the music and the sound of typing. And though I dutifully stared at the empty sheet before me, I couldn't write a word.

♦ ♦ ♦

I was lying in bed with my eyes wide open when the phone rang the next morning. "It's for you," Body called out, tapping softly on the door. I got out of bed, pulled my pants on, and went into the kitchen. The receiver was lying speaker end up on the tabletop. "Hello?" I said. It was Tammy.

"Are you all right?" she asked.

"I'm fine," I told her. "How are you?"

"How am I?" she half laughed, half screamed.

"Yeah. How are things going?" I said, hoping to calm her down. One thing about Tammy, she'd always tended toward irrational emotional outbursts. Sometimes, for example, she burst out crying for no apparent reason whatsoever.

"Look, Roger, have you flipped out completely? Pull yourself together. I'm here at the airport."

"Airport? What airport? What are you talking about?"

"San Sebastian airport. I just arrived. Should I take a taxi or can you arrange to pick me up?"

"San Sebastian?" I repeated. "But what are you doing here?"

"What do you mean, what am I doing here?" she huffed into the phone. "When you called yesterday you were on the verge of a nervous breakdown. You all but begged me to come rescue you from this maniac cult figure who's holding you captive, drugging and brainwashing you. So I dropped everything and called your parents, who, by the way, are really worried, too. Your dad was just about to leave on a business trip to Los Angeles, but he's got a really important meeting there today he can't miss, so he bought me a ticket to San Sebastian and said he'd rent a car in L.A. and drive up here as soon as he gets out of his meeting."

"Christ, Tammy, you've got to be kidding. Isn't everyone overreacting a bit?"

"Hardly, Roger. If anyone was overreacting, it was you yesterday on the phone. You were crying almost the whole time, blubbering, in fact, weeping and carrying on so hysterically that I could hardly understand half of what you said."

I sat down in one of the dinette chairs. "You'd better take a taxi," I told her. She said she'd be there in fifteen minutes and hung up so quickly the dial tone hummed in my ear.

"Everything okay?" Body asked, as I carefully replaced the phone in its cradle on the wall. He was wearing the terrycloth robe again. I tried not to stare.

"My girlfriend happens to be in the area and might stop by sometime today as well," I said, "if that's okay with you."

"Sure thing, Roger, the more the merrier," Body said, cheerfully. He seemed to be enjoying himself and his smile was beginning to irritate me. When he turned his back, I thought of putting my hands around his neck, throwing him to the floor and choking him. But I realized that would only provide him with another story. He turned back toward me and set a cup of coffee down before me on the table. "You want a piece of toast?" he asked. I shook my head no and asked for a towel instead.

"I should take a shower before she gets here," I explained. He looked me over and nodded.

"A shower can change the course of a person's life," he said, gravely. Behind him two pieces of bread popped out of the toaster and into the air.

I'd just finished shaving and had taken a seat in the living room when I saw the white Toyota with the dented side panel pull up in front of the house. I watched as Tammy, dressed in jeans, a university sweatshirt and sunglasses, pulled a suitcase from the back seat and dragged it across the lawn. Then I got up and went to open the door.

I met her on the stoop. Though she set her luggage down, we didn't kiss, hug or even shake hands. Her lips seemed thin and I couldn't see her eyes. "Hello," I said, but she didn't answer. Instead she stood staring at me through her dark lenses, her arms crossed over her chest. I was wondering which one of us would be the first to burst into tears when Body threw open the door and broke the silence.

"Hi there," he said to Tammy, extending his hand. Fortunately, he'd put on a pair of corduroy pants and a work shirt. A cigarette dangled from his mouth. "I'm George Body, and your name is?" He looked over at me.

The Conference

"I'm sorry," I mumbled, "George, this is Tammy Shackman. Tammy, my writing teacher George Body." They shook hands and George turned to me.

"Sorry to interrupt, Roger, but you've got another phone call. Your father, I think he said it was."

I left the two of them on the doorstep and headed straight for the kitchen. As I walked, I realized that the closer I got to the phone, the faster and shallower my breathing was becoming. I steadied myself against the wall and picked the receiver up off the table. "Hello," I said.

"Roger, is that you?"

"Yes, dad."

"Listen, son, sounds like you've got yourself into a bit of a mess up there."

"I suppose," I said.

"Did Tammy get there okay?"

"She's here now."

"Good. I've got to go into a meeting in five minutes and a lot is riding on our presentation here, but I'll be up as soon as I can."

"Dad, I really don't think . . ."

"Listen, Roger, just stay put and don't do anything stupid. I'll straighten everything out when I get there this evening. Now could you put Tammy on the line?"

"Sure thing," I said, and set the receiver back down on the table. I opened the refrigerator, got two beers out, and opened them, then carried them outside to where George was showing Tammy God-knows-what kind of weed that was growing in the planter in front of the house. "Tammy, my dad wants to talk to you," I said. I handed George one of the bottles and put the other to my lips. I'd never been so thirsty.

"Another visitor?" George asked. I nodded. We sipped our beers in silence. After a while George excused himself and went back into the house. "We'll talk later," he said.

When I'd finished drinking my beer, I tossed the bottle into the weeds and walked to the corner, where I sat down on a concrete and wood bench. Several minutes later a bus stopped and I boarded it, fishing in my pocket for change. I got off at a shopping mall a couple of miles up the road.

Inside, I spent a long time wandering around the department stores. I went to the men's clothing section of one and tried on a dress shirt, tie and sports coat. I sought out a store that specialized in luggage and asked to see several briefcases, browsed the classical section of a music store, sat down to eat a hotdog and drank a coke. For dessert I bummed a cigarette. For a long time I simply sat and listened to the conversations of people sitting close by. On the next bench a little boy was having lunch with his mother. They were eating hamburgers and the kid wanted to throw the beef patty away and eat just the bun. Though his mother pleaded with him, he refused to eat the hamburger. For a few minutes the kid stared off into the distance, holding the burger in his lap. When his mother tried to touch him on the shoulder, he shook away from her hand. Then she grabbed the burger from him, threw it into the trashcan and pulled him roughly up by the arm. They left with her tugging him toward the nearest exit.

I got up and went into a stationary store, where I bought a lined yellow pad of paper and a ballpoint pen. Then I sat back down and began writing a story called "Meat Dreams" about a seven-year-old kid who keeps waking up screaming in the middle of the night. He tells his parents that he's been dreaming about raw meat—in the dream his bed is full of cold steaks and chickens cut into pieces, his pillow turned to ground round that presses against his cheek. It's a recurring nightmare, one he's had every night for the past week. His parents take him to a child psychologist who asks both the mother and the father, each in turn, privately, a number of embarrassing and personal questions about

The Conference

their sex life. At one point the mother breaks down and cries. "It's so awful, so disgusting," she says.

But the story went nowhere and after a few pages I gave up and went into a bookstore to ask if they had any books by George Body. None of the clerks had ever heard of him before, so I asked to speak to the manager, who pushed at her glasses and told me that to her knowledge there were no writers living in San Sebastian. She even laughed at the idea. I demanded she look up the name in *Books in Print* and when she found six titles listed, I got out my wallet and told her I wanted to special order them all. "We don't do that here," she said. "You'll have to go to a full-service bookstore."

I took off wandering again and somehow ended up in the lingerie section of another big department store. Two sales clerks there were standing with their hands on their hips and talking in high, excited voices. From time to time they looked down the aisle with creased faces. When I followed their gaze, I saw an old man waltzing in a corner with a mannequin dressed in a white corset adorned with tiny red bows. I watched as two young security officers arrived and gently dragged him away. As they passed by me I saw that he was crying.

As I left the mall, the sky was already darkening, the sun slipping over the mountains in the distance. I started walking. Along the way I threw the pad with "Meat Dreams" into a trash can someone had left on the curb.

◆ ◆ ◆

By the time I got back to the house there were two rental cars parked on the street in front. When I opened the door I was surprised to find Tammy, Dr. Harder, my father, and George Body all sitting together in the living room. They were drinking beer and listening closely as Dr. Harder, who was sitting on one of the dinette chairs that had been moved to form a circle with the couch and armchair, read aloud from a sheaf of manuscript pages. George sat in the armchair, his beer between his legs, a stack of papers at his feet. My father and Tammy were sitting together on the couch and there was a pink school notebook and a laptop computer on the coffee table before them. I couldn't help from remarking that Dad had slipped his arm around Tammy's shoulder. As I stood in the foyer and took in the scene, I slowly realized that Body had persuaded them all to participate in the writer's conference and they had started the session without me.

The four of them were so engrossed by what they were doing that they hardly paused to acknowledge my presence. For a second Harder stopped reading, as George moved another dinette chair in from the kitchen and asked me to sit down. Then the reading continued. I learned later that the piece Harder was reading was entitled "Sardines." He'd written it especially to present to student writers at the Norwich Avenue Fiction Writers Symposium in San Francisco. I listened carefully as the professor continued:

"Then one day he thought to himself that he'd like nothing better than to fuck his neighbor's wife. And who could blame him? She was young, fresh, attractive, friendly, intelligent, sexy, maternal, coquettish, straightforward, innocent and worldly. She was also a marvelous cook. Moreover, she was almost dizzyingly voluptuous and had a habit of hanging black lace bras with huge cup sizes on the clothesline in her backyard. So he sat down and wrote out the whole seduction, making it clear to any reader, including potential judges and jurors, that the affair had been initiated by Sylvia, who had come to his house to borrow a cup of sugar, followed him into his kitchen, and wrapped her arms, and not much

later her legs as well, around him. By the time he stood up from his word processor, he had reached several orgasms, including one via a procedure new to him, though imagined often. It had been, he admitted to himself, the most significant sexual experience of his life. He sighed and sat back down at the keyboard to write about smoking a cigarette.

"After such impassioned loving he soon felt his appetite building. Specifically, he craved sardines in tomato sauce, which he described in loving detail, from the shiny tin with the silver, red and black label, to the sound of the tin creaking open as the key turned, to the heady smell of the fish themselves, to the distinct flavor of saltfish, oil, and tangy tomatoes, to the crunchy popping of the spines between his teeth. He savored every word.

"When I'd finished reading the story, I knew Jeremy was onto something, but I wasn't sure I liked it. He'd always been one for taking chance with his writing, but somehow I felt this time he was going too far.

"The last time I saw Jeremy he was pale and terribly thin. He hadn't left his apartment for months and some of us were getting worried and had stopped by to see for ourselves just how bad things had turned. 'I'm feeling great,' Jeremy told us, 'Been lifting weights, running marathons, eating three-plus squares a day, making love to the most beautiful women in the world, sailing yachts, breaking out of prison, racing cars, fighting bare-knuckle bouts for big prize money, gunning down crooked politicians, winning wars, shooting elephants, climbing trees, exploring rivers, catching fish, smoking cigars and eating lots of sardines. I got nothing to complain about.' When he smiled, I could see how few teeth were left hanging loose in his mouth.

"They buried my friend Jeremy last week, while I was still abroad. I read about his passing in the **international** edition of the Herald Tribune. 'One of the most promising writers of his generation,' the obituary had read. When I *got back home I pulled his last collection of stories from the shelf and reread 'Sardines.' When I was done I turned back to the beginning and read through it again. And then again. I gorged myself on 'Sardines' until the words rose in my throat and spewed forth into the toilet."*

After Dr. Harder finished reading, the room remained quiet for a moment as he shuffled the papers and busied himself, tapping them square against his knee. Finally George Body cleared his throat and began talking. "Hey, Sam, that's an interesting piece—a real guy-going-to-extremes bit. It reminds me a little of "The Hunger Artist." But I enjoyed it nonetheless. I do have a couple of suggestions, though. First, take yourself out of the narrative. I can do without the moralistic frame, and as a reader I really don't much care about that first-person narrator, as he sounds like a snob, a toady and an all-around bore. It's Jeremy that we want to hear about. His mind creates and the other guy pukes. Second, I'm wondering why there are no decapitations in the piece. Keep in mind that fiction is itself disembodied. Anyway, nice job, Sam. Keep writing. Next let's hear from Tammy." George opened his palm and pointed toward her by way of an introduction.

Tammy picked up her pink-covered notebook and opened it to a page she'd marked with a pen near the center. "For the past couple of months I've been writing stories," she said in a quiet voice. She glanced up at me and then returned her gaze quickly to her notebook. "I started after reading some of what Roger was writing. I don't know, I just figured I could do better. You know what I mean?" She shrugged her shoulders. "Anyway, I haven't told anybody I was doing it or let anyone read my stories before, so I'm kind of nervous. But here goes. This is my latest. It's called 'The Tomboy'."

The Conference

"Maria Wolcroft had been raised as the youngest child among five older brothers. So it was only natural that she spent much of her childhood imitating her siblings. Throughout her early years she dressed in the same overalls, jeans and t-shirts as her brothers. According to season, she played basketball, hockey, football or baseball. She shot BB guns and slingshots, fired cap guns, shot arrows with bows. She climbed trees, sawed and hammered, helped built forts and tunnels. She blew the lids off of metal trashcans with cherry bombs, hunted for lizards and snakes. And she cried whenever her mother brushed out her hair and made her wear a dress.

"All the mothers in the neighborhood would shake their heads and call her 'Tomboy,' and the other little girls would stay away from her if they could. 'She's too rough,' they'd complain when she broke their dolls or got dirt on their white dresses. Once a new girl at school made the mistake of teasing Maria about playing kickball with the boys during recess and Maria made her pay with a bloody nose. The school principal made it clear to Maria's mother that her daughter was far from ladylike. 'It's not the kind of behavior we've come to expect from our girls,' he said.

"For a month Maria was forced to stay indoors and help with chores around the house. Her mother ushered her from one activity to the next, guiding her carefully through a series of sewing lessons and teaching her how to knit a muffler. She even helped her experiment with cosmetics. Maria baked cookies, read books about nurses and clever girl detectives, practiced kicking field goals with a Barbi Doll. It was the worst month of her life.

"By the time Maria's breasts began to sprout and her menstrual cycle commenced, she'd become adept at wearing the disguise of womanhood. Though she still scrimmaged with her brothers and their companions on the playing fields, she also found friends among the girls, and spent equal time standing around in their giggling groups at school. She went to slumber parties and talked about boys. Unlike the other girls, she knew the coarse feel of masculine hands against her body. Her friends laughed and blushed as she described how they'd tackled her from behind and pushed themselves on top of her before rolling off on the football field.

"In high school Maria blossomed into a lovely princess. Her breasts swelled up large and round, jiggling high on her chest, and her hips and buttocks widened in her jeans. When she walked across the campus she could see the boys following her with their eyes. A star athlete on the girls basketball, softball and track teams, Maria was also elected homecoming queen. But now the boys she'd played with only a few years earlier avoided her, lowering their eyes when she came into a room, stumbling over their words when she joked with them in the cafeteria at lunch.

"On her first date an older boy from the senior class took her to a drive-in movie, where he slid his arm around her and leaned over to give her a kiss. After a couple of minutes he placed his hand on her breast. By then he was shaking so violently she thought he might have a seizure. 'What's wrong?' she asked.

"'You're so beautiful,' he said, 'it's driving me crazy.'

"Maria felt a bit tingly and breathless herself. 'We'd better watch the movie,' she said, finally.

"After the boy had dropped her off at home, Maria asked her brothers why her date had started shaking. They laughed and said the poor guy was just horny. 'He's got the bluest balls in the county right now,' one of them told her and they all laughed again. 'He probably jerked off in his car as soon as you left,' piped in another brother. Then one of them made a back and forth motion with his fist and the four of them doubled over in laughter.

"That night in bed Maria began thinking about penises. Her family had never been particularly shy about nudity, so

The Conference

she'd seen her brothers' sexual organs dozens of times over the years as they got into or out of the shower or dressed for the beach, and she knew technically from her Health class what they were used for. Still, she'd never given much thought to the fact that they were centers of pleasurable sensation. She thought of the jerky fist her brother had made and imagined wrapping her hand around a turgid column of sensitive flesh.

"Her mind full of thoughts about erect male organs, she slowly let her hand drift up under her nightshirt until she felt a warm wetness between her legs. She raised her knees and spread her legs wide, then moved her hand in a circular motion until her fingers were wet and sliding around the labia of her vagina. She started breathing faster and her pulse rate increased. She let her fingers travel upward and gasped out loud as she touched the inch-long stem of her erect clitoris. She made a tight circle with her forefinger and thumb and massaged the bulb, jerking her hand roughly with the same motion her brother had made. Giddy with pleasure, she rolled onto her stomach and pressed her erection against the palm of her hand, rocking her hips until she shuddered in waves, screaming into her pillow.

"Maria kept her virginity until her second year of college, where, now a cheerleader herself, she met a young man, a team-mate of one of her brothers on the basketball squad, who melted her heart with his good looks and awesome ball-handling skills. They made love for the first time in the dark, after a victory celebration for the win over State, and she thought she'd die from the pleasure of the rhythmic pounding of his muscular pelvis and stomach against her own tiny penis. But he'd been so excited that he'd only lasted a few quick strokes, and as he rolled off her, she lay in bed with her own erection still throbbing.

"'Baby, I need to come,' she told him, and reached over to switch on the light. Then she spread her legs and guided *his head between them. 'Suck my cock,' she said to him. It was the greatest thing that ever happened to her."*

Tammy sighed, then closed the notebook and set it back down on the coffee table before her.

"Oh for Christ's sake, Tammy," I blurted out, "that's absurd. What would drive you to write such a pile of pornographic garbage?"

"I think it's really very good," my father said, patting Tammy on the knee. I noticed he didn't remove his hand when he'd finished the patting and that Tammy moved to cover it with her own.

"Thanks, Dick," she said, and smiled at him. "I'm sorry you don't appreciate it, Roger," she spat back at me, her voice sharp as broken glass.

I rolled my eyes and looked at Dr. Harder, who was smiling hugely, his legs crossed. He winked back at me.

"At least she got the head in there," said George.

Next my father read a story off his laptop computer. "It's a little parable I wrote on the plane. I was going to print it out and give it to Roger," he explained, putting on his reading glasses. "I've entitled it 'The Senator from Rome.' " He leaned forward to squint at the backlit crystal screen and began reading:

"In ancient Rome there lived a man named Marcus Aurelius Industrius, a man who had, through life's standard misfortune, been born a slave and spent his youth in the salt mines of Sardinia. Through his strength, his intelligence, and his great cunning and undeniable capability he won promotion after promotion until he'd been appointed foreman by the owner of the mine. One day while the owner and his slave foreman were touring one of the new tunnels one of the support beams gave out, trapping them underground. The owner, a flabby nobleman who'd never done a day's work in his

The Conference

life, immediately collapsed on the ground and began renting his clothes. 'The gods have forsaken us,' he cried out. But Marcus did not despair. Instead, he began digging with his bare hands. He dug until his fingers were bleeding, laughing to himself at the cowardly sobs of the nobleman. After a great effort he succeeded in digging through the rubble of the collapsed tunnel, thus rescuing the owner, who promptly rewarded him with his freedom.

"'From this day forth, you are no longer a slave, but my son,' said the owner. He took him to his villa and gave him a purple toga. In time the owner died from some combination of overeating and venereal disease brought on by deviant sexual practices, leaving Marcus ownership of the mine, several choice olive groves and a very pleasant country estate. But our hero was not content to live out his life as a gentleman of independent means. Taking stock of his holdings, he immediately began a program of shrewd yet cautious investments, supplying not only salt, but iron spear tips for the conquering legions of Rome.

"In time he married a local but solid woman of noble stock and began a family. A son was born unto him and he offered sacrifice in honor of the gods. This son, whom he named Athleticus, grew to be a wrestler of great promise. Throughout the land he was honored for his strength and natural gifts, so much so, in fact, that his father agreed to favor him with his financial support whilst he ventured to Rome, where he would train with the great athletic masters and compete for the honor of his family name. And so it was that young Athleticus kissed his mother, embraced his father firmly around the shoulders, and left to seek his fortune.

"Soon after, Marcus Aurelius Industrius himself was called to Rome, for he'd been honored for his achievements and leadership abilities with election to the Senate. There he heard reports of his son's activities that disturbed him. It seems Athleticus had fallen under the influence of a wicked

Greek rhymester, a poet of little repute who, concerned only for his own personal gain, had persuaded Athleticus to pay him for instruction in the art of versification. This Greek, who went by the name of Sophisiticus, was a thoroughly decadent and unclean fellow, the kind of human scum that gums up the works of society with his chicken-shit liberal socialism, his twisted sentiment, and his artistic pretensions. And alas, poor Marcus Aurelius was despondent to find how thoroughly Athleticus had been duped.

"After making the usual inquiries, he learned that his son had been neglecting his coach's instructions, missing practice sessions at the gymnasium, and deporting himself in a most ignoble manner whilst carousing with the Greek and his poetic associates. They'd been seen together declaiming verse in the public baths and in the company of unworthy women of the lowest social order, women who rented their favors for a place at the table. All of this was unsettling, nay, unbearable, to the new senator. His son had shamed him, disgraced his good name, and made a mockery of the values he represented.

"The senator sought out his unworthy son and found him lying in a shadowy hovel, in neglect of his training, and suffering from the unhealthful abuses of bad living. He appeared to him as a mere shadow of his former self. 'Son, all this poetry is fine and good, providing one has a sponsor. Art is, after all, mere entertainment, a pleasant enough diversion for the affluent. But you who have no other means of support . . . Surely you don't mean to sell yourself as the means by which to prop up the vanity of some petty merchant who wishes his life celebrated in verse?' But though the father employed every argument of logic and reason and ended in a heartfelt plea for his son to mend his ways, to give up once and for all his unworthy ambition, Athleticus, drunk on unwatered wine and seduced by the sound of the

The Conference

lyre, refused to listen, insisting that his verses would find favor and win him, in time, immortality.

"Marcus Aurelius wandered back to his chambers in an advanced state of anger and grief. All around him the streets of Rome teemed with scenes of decadence and unspeakable filth. It seemed to him the values he'd struggled so hard to preserve were crumbling around him. The once-proud and strong Roman soul had succumbed to the illusion of an easy life, a life of pleasure and frivolity. And while excesses of the orgy rooms and vomitoriums threatened the very fabric of society, here was his own flesh and blood, a young man with much promise, a future leader, off penning verses about love. 'It's my fault,' he said to himself, 'I've been too easy on him, too indulgent. That's not the Roman way.'

"There seemed but one course of action open to him. When he arrived at the senate, he called forth a centurion and gave him orders to arrest his son. 'A couple years in the salt mines will do him good,' he said to one of his colleagues. But by that time it was too late. The Goths, Vandals, Visigoths, Huns, and Japanese were already storming the city, killing, plundering, and raping as they advanced. 'The glory days are over,' said the Senator, as he plunged downward onto his sword."

I was too angry at the time to remember much about the specific responses to my father's story, except that Tammy had cried out, "Oh Dick, that's wonderful," and threw her arms around his neck. I recall that I simply sat in silence with my back perfectly straight in the chair and looked out the window, as the others commented, one after the next. At some point my eyes focused on a man across the street who appeared to be slapping around a young woman. During this time I believe Dr. Harder made some general comments about the decline of respect for institutions, then launched into a lecture on the quality of students and educational standards currently as compared to twenty years previous when he was a student. A bowl of pretzels circulated around the room and I grabbed a handful and chewed them mechanically, as the voices and laughter around me turned into a dull hum. Across the street the police arrived in force. I watched as one set of officers handcuffed the man and pushed him headfirst into the back seat of a squad car while another interviewed the victim.

Suddenly I became aware of someone calling my name. I looked around at the faces staring at me. When George asked if I had anything to read to the group, I lowered my head and said no. "Well, then, I guess this little charade is over," my father said. He pulled an airline ticket from his shirt pocket and waved it in the air. "Get your stuff together and let's get the hell out of here. Tammy's suitcase is already in the trunk."

"I'm not going anywhere until I've written something," I told him. "I'll take the bus back when I'm done." My father threw his hands up in the air.

"Oh, for Christ's sake, grow up," he snorted. He blew a loud puff of disgust through his mouth as he snapped his portable computer case shut. The party was over. Everyone got up to leave.

"Rotten luck," said Dr. Harder.

My father shook his head sadly. "I think you're going to regret this, son," he said, walking toward the door. Tammy followed behind him, taking her sunglasses from her purse. As they moved across the lawn toward the rental car, she slipped her arm around my father's waist. "Goodbye, Roger," she called back over her shoulder. I stood in the doorway and watched them drive away, Harder in his red sports car and my father and girlfriend in a rented Cadillac. No one bothered to wave. When I came back into the kitchen George was brewing coffee.

"Don't worry, kid, conferences can be like that."

The Conference

"Like *what?*" I wanted to say, but the words were stuck somewhere in my throat.

"You've just had your head filled up with other people's stories again," he said. I pointed my chin toward my room and he nodded.

For the next couple of days I worked steadily, pounding at the keys of the typewriter, pausing only to use the bathroom, to walk around the block, to sleep, and to eat and drink whatever leftovers I found in the refrigerator. Instead of making something up, I wrote a story about what had just happened. When I was done I gathered up the sheets of paper and laid them, like a head on a plate, on the kitchen table.

I looked for George, but of course he was long gone.